NEWARK PUBLIC LIBRARY-NEWARK, OHIO 43055

3 2487 00785 7049

WITHDRAWN

Large Print Wes
Weston, Sophie.
The accidental mistress

STACKS

W9-BUG-813

THE ACCIDENTAL
MISTRESS

THE ACCIDENTAL MISTRESS

BY

SOPHIE WESTON

MILLS & BOON®

All the characters in this book have no existence outside the imagination of the author, and have no relation whatsoever to anyone bearing the same name or names. They are not even distantly inspired by any individual known or unknown to the author, and all the incidents are pure invention.

All Rights Reserved including the right of reproduction in whole or in part in any form. This edition is published by arrangement with Harlequin Enterprises II B.V. The text of this publication or any part thereof may not be reproduced or transmitted in any form or by any means, electronic or mechanical, including photocopying, recording, storage in an information retrieval system, or otherwise, without the written permission of the publisher.

MILLS & BOON and
MILLS & BOON with the Rose Device
are registered trademarks of the publisher.

First published in Great Britain 2003
Large Print edition 2004
Harlequin Mills & Boon Limited,
Eton House, 18-24 Paradise Road,
Richmond, Surrey TW9 1SR

© Sophie Weston 2003

ISBN 0 263 18055 7

Set in Times Roman 15½ on 16¾ pt.
16-0304-55300

Printed and bound in Great Britain
by Antony Rowe Ltd, Chippenham, Wiltshire

Large Print Wes
Weston, Sophie.
The accidental mistress

7857049

PROLOGUE

'WE'RE missing the Wow! factor here, people,' said the senior account executive of Culp and Christopher Public Relations. 'There's nothing special about explorers. Explorers are *everywhere*.'

Dominic Templeton-Burke was sitting opposite him, doodling impatiently. But at this he raised his head and stared in disbelief. His handsome bony face seemed to freeze for a moment, and then he gave a gulp that just might—if C&C weren't the most famous PR agency in London and doing this for free—have been a choked laugh.

'It goes with the job description, I'm afraid,' he said in a strangled voice.

The senior account executive was not used to being laughed at and did not recognise it now. He gave a tolerant smile. 'Can't be helped. But what we have to ask ourselves here is—what makes Dominic Templeton-Burke *unique*?'

There was a pause.

5

NEWARK PUBLIC LIBRARY
NEWARK, OHIO 43055-5054

'He's sexy?' offered emerald-haired ebony-nailed Molly di Peretti at last. She sounded doubtful.

This time Dominic did not even try to hide his grin. 'Gee, thanks,' he murmured.

None of the PR professionals took any notice. They felt some sympathy for Molly. Normally she dealt with rock musicians, and the rangy adventurer was proving a challenge. Oh, he was good-looking enough. He just didn't take it seriously—and hadn't from the moment Managing Director Jay Christopher had said, 'This is Dom. He's going for a stroll in the Arctic and has just lost ten per cent of his funding. We're going to help.'

But helping Dom Templeton-Burke was turning out to be an uphill struggle.

Except that senior account executives didn't notice! 'All explorers are sexy,' said the senior account executive loftily.

His subordinates exchanged weary glances.

'They are,' he insisted. 'It goes with all that heaving backpacks around and lack of aftershave. Pure testosterone. We need that something extra.'

It was undeniable. There was silence while they all thought.

'Something to show his sensitive side?' hazarded Josh, newly out of his training course.

Dominic lost his grin. 'Not too sensitive,' he said firmly.

His sister Abby, an account executive in her own right, glared down the table at him. Only threats of major family recrimination had got her reluctant brother here this morning and she was watching him like a hawk.

'Try to be constructive, Dom.' She'd meant to be crisp. Too late, she heard the pleading note in her voice. She could have kicked herself.

Dominic was her favourite brother, but she had never tried to interfere with his professional life before. It was turning out to be an unforgettable experience.

'We're trying to help you here,' she said, in despair.

'Sorry.' But he did not sound repentant. And his grey green eyes were dancing. He sat back. 'What had you in mind?'

The account executive waved a vague hand. 'Something quirky. Something unexpected. Something people will remember. I'm looking for the human face here.'

'You mean something that says there's more to you than muscles and the ability to read a compass,' said his fond sister maliciously.

Dominic flicked a paper pellet at her.

'He means the man of mystery behind my rough, tough exterior,' he corrected. 'We're talking swirling cloaks and stirred martinis. Probably with a glamorous mistress thrown in,' he added wickedly.

There was sudden, total silence. The staff of Culp and Christopher exchanged startled glances.

They had heard about Abby's brother. He might not be a bad and brooding rock star. But, between expeditions, he partied enthusiastically. In fact, in the folders in front of them, Molly's briefing concluded, 'The word on the street is that he's brilliant, unpredictable and an all-round awkward sod. Does the full male on the loose thing— then disappears to go into training without a word. Sexually a stud. Socially a blast. Romantically a bad, *bad* bet.'

'Er,' said Molly, trying not to look at her folder.

Even Abby, who had not seen the briefing— well, he was her brother after all—looked uncomfortable.

'Ho yus?' she said with heavy irony. 'Like you'd remember you had a hot babe waiting for you when someone was offering to show you some marvellous new bit of climbing equipment?'

Dominic's eyes twinkled. 'You're saying I'm not sexy again,' he said sadly.

Every woman at the table looked at him with professional assessment. Beneath the careless clothing the tall rangy body was powerfully muscled. Only that wicked teasing meant that you never quite knew where you were with him. He would be a challenge, but...

'I'm saying you should have *No Involvement* tattooed on your forehead,' snapped Abby, goaded. 'Are you telling me I'm wrong?'

'I thought I was here for PR advice. Not character assassination.'

Was he annoyed? Looking at those wicked green eyes, no one round the table could be sure.

Molly di Peretti said hastily, 'A high-profile flirtation could get us some coverage, sure. But—' She looked at Abby for a lead.

Abby was passing a list of his most recent girl-friends under rapid review. To a woman they were gorgeous, sweet-tempered and pliant. And temporary. No sign that Dominic wanted to abandon his detachment, as far as she could see. Still—he really needed that funding. There was a *chance* that it was a serious suggestion.

She cleared her throat. 'Have you got anyone in mind?'

Dom opened his eyes very wide. 'Me? Isn't that your job? That's what I thought you people got paid for.' He sounded injured—and very innocent.

Abby knew that tone. Serious? Not a hope! She could have screamed. Or thrown her folder at his mischievous head.

'Hmm,' said the senior account executive, oblivious of undercurrents. 'It's a thought. It's definitely a thought.'

Abby knew that her brother was winding them up, even if her colleagues had missed it. 'Not a good idea at all,' she said crisply. 'Madame de Pompadour is not currently on our books. Besides, Dom's girlfriend wouldn't like it at all— whoever she is at the moment,' she added acidly.

Dominic sent her an amused look. 'No girlfriend currently on board,' he said blandly. 'I'm open to offers.'

'I like it,' decided the senior account executive. 'We could definitely do something with that.'

Dom nodded enthusiastically. 'What have you in mind?' he said with flattering attention.

Abby groaned.

Dominic ignored her. 'Something gorgeous and blonde with legs to her eyebrows?' he said hopefully.

Abby dropped her head in her hands.

The senior account executive, less alert than Abby, gave an impatient wave of the hand.

'Don't bother you with details, huh?' Dominic smiled with apparent sympathy. 'Yeah, I know the feeling. People will fuss about the unimportant stuff, won't they?'

But, lifting her head, Abby saw that his eyes were dancing in a way that she knew all too well.

'Dom—' she began warningly.

As if she hadn't spoken, Dominic leaned forward and put his elbows on the boardroom table. He steepled his fingers and rested his chin on them. He was the picture of intelligent co-operation. Abby distrusted him deeply.

'You're getting a lot of advice for free. Don't waste it,' she advised him curtly. Without much hope. When something appealed to his sense of humour Dom was unstoppable. 'Get serious,' she finished despairingly.

He turned limpid eyes on her. 'Serious? Honestly, Abby, I can see the idea has a lot going for it.' He beamed round the table. 'Just fill me in a bit. I mean, it was just an idea off the top of my head. I haven't thought it through. Do you really think a mistress will spruce up my public image? And where do you think I should get one?'

Abby gave up. 'Rent-a-Bird?' she muttered sourly.

Dominic slapped her lightly under the table. 'Ignore her. Come on, ladies and gentlemen. Remember, I'm just a simple country boy who doesn't know his way around big city public relations. Walk me through this one.'

Abby cast her eyes to the ceiling.

'Dom, *stop* this.'

But the senior account executive could not imagine a client teasing him.

'Sex sells,' he explained seriously. He was quite kind, but his tone said that Dom knew even less about real life than the newly employed Josh.

'Ah,' said Dom, still mild. 'But we're selling my next expedition, right? Um, sorry chaps, this may be new to you. But there's not a lot of sex at the South Pole.'

The senior account executive was patient. 'All the more reason why you need some in the PR campaign.'

That was too much for Dominic. His wicked control snapped at last. He gave a hoot of laughter and buried his head in his hands.

'You're mad,' he said, when he could speak. 'Absolutely out of your tree, every man jack of you. PR obviously rots the brain.'

He stood up and looked round the table.

'Thanks for the offer of help,' he said. 'I know you meant it kindly. Think I'll pass, all the same.'

He walked out, still chuckling.

He left silence behind him.

Then Molly drew a long, satisfied breath. 'Unpredictable,' she said, pleased with her research. 'Told you so.'

Abby bit her lip. 'I'm so sorry…'

Molly patted her hand. 'That's okay. We'll tell Jay we gave it our best shot and Dom wouldn't play. No problem. Even Jay can't force the man to take on a PR package.' She chuckled suddenly. 'Though I must say I rather fancy setting him up with Madame de Pompadour. Sorry to be mean about your brother, Abby, but he could do with a crash course in respect.'

Abby winced. If it weren't for family loyalty she would have cheered.

People gathered up their papers and pushed back their chairs, ready to move on to a more promising assignment.

Only the senior account executive still had something to say. He was not offended but his tone was wistful.

'It would have made a great story. Think of the headlines. *A man's man and his lucky lady!*' He met the appalled eyes of his female colleagues and came back to earth. 'With the right woman, of course. Only with the right woman.'

Abby and Molly exchanged eloquent glances.

'The right woman?' echoed Molly, incredulous. 'You think there's a right woman for Dominic Templeton-Burke?'

Loyalty lost the battle. 'Fat chance,' said Abby.

CHAPTER ONE

IT WAS one of those crisp clear late summer mornings that said autumn was coming. Isabel Dare, doing her stretches just inside the park gates, drew deep, luxuriating breaths. Peace, she thought.

Alone. Room to breathe. Silence to think, except for the birds twittering in the trees. For the first time in weeks, *months*, there was no one walking her off the pavement as if she didn't exist. No stifling underground train with a stranger's elbow in her side and her nose pressed into someone else's back. No beep announcing the next text message.

Just not a natural London person, I guess, she told herself wryly.

The next text message would be, like all the others, from Adam. She knew what it would say. 'Date 3 whn?'

The problem was, she didn't know the answer.

'Third date coming up, huh?' Jemima had said last night, just before she dropped her overnight flight bag and crashed. 'Hope he has more luck than the last five. I like Adam.'

Well, Izzy liked him, too. She just wasn't sure she wanted him to move in any closer. And the third date was—well, *big*.

Bigger even than she'd realised, thought Izzy wryly now. She and Jemima called it the Sex Date. They always had; it was a sister thing. So Izzy was taken aback to find that everyone else seemed to be calling it the Sex Date, too. Including Adam Sadler.

He was getting increasingly impatient, too. To be honest, Izzy couldn't blame him. The trouble was, it wasn't just London that was getting her down. Adam—and the five guys before him—were a big part of it, too. She enjoyed dating; she liked having a good time. But she didn't want to go through the third date barrier with any of them. Not any more.

She took herself to task. Well, maybe make that not with anyone *yet*. Things could change. Meanwhile—

Izzy shook her head. 'Hard-Hearted Hannah,' she said with a grin. 'They'll just have to live with it.'

She began to jog quietly along the grass beside the Tarmac path. It was only just six-thirty, but already the sky was hazy with the promise of heat. It would be a perfect day for walking in the woods. Or canoeing. Or just lazing by the river

under the shade of a willow, watching the insects
hover and thinking of nothing. Alone.

'Not an option,' she said aloud, squashing regret.

Today was her cousin Pepper's big day. Today
saw the opening of *Out of the Attic*, Pepper's new
retail concept. Pepper had put her heart and soul
into this, her breakout venture on her own, and
Izzy had worked with her on it for months. This
was a day of presentations and schmoozing and
parties. No time for willows.

Izzy sighed—but she laughed as well.

The trouble was, she thought, Pepper really
cared about shopping. Whereas Izzy didn't, not if
she were honest. Still, that didn't matter. Pepper
had given her a job when she'd been so badly
shaken she'd thought that she was unemployable
and always would be.

Not that Pepper knew that. Nobody did. Izzy
had taken good care of that. Izzy fought her de-
mons in private. Always had.

She increased her pace.

The low morning sun struck rainbows off of
the dew-wet leaves. Birds sang. A heron cruised
idly over the mill-pond surface of the lake. It was
not really hunting, just checking out the scene,
she thought with a grin.

The exercise was beginning to take effect.
Izzy's blood pumped and her skin tingled. Oh,

this felt good. This would make up for the hours to come. Hours of monitoring what she said to make sure she stayed on message; of circulating in air thick with warring perfumes; of feeling that she was drowning in people.

When she'd first moved to London she'd run in the park every day. Always early, very early, when it was virtually deserted.

'But isn't that terribly dangerous?' New Yorker Pepper had said, blenching, the first time she met Izzy in the hallway in her shorts and running shoes.

Izzy laughed. 'I run fast and I kick hard.'

'She does,' agreed Jemima with a grin. Jemima had been there all the time then. Hadn't got her big job; wasn't travelling twenty-four days a month; still *listened*.

But Pepper was unconvinced. 'But what if a man came at you with a gun?'

Inwardly Izzy tensed. But outwardly she stayed unconcerned. She shrugged. 'Run if you can. If you can't—negotiate!'

Jemima, still in silky kimono with a coffee in her hand, shook her head at her cousin.

'That's what she always says, Pepper. Izzy has been all round the world you know. Every time she comes back without a scratch. So she must be right.'

Pepper was unconvinced. 'But the risk!'

Izzy was unlacing her shoes, but at that she turned her head and said with quite unnecessary force, 'Life is all about risks.' She eased the shoes off, sat on the polished parquet and looked up at the other two. 'Run away from one and you just rush slap into another. So you can either sit in a locked room and shiver. Or take the risks. And learn to deal with the consequences.' Her voice was hard.

Pepper, who was in the middle of the biggest risk of her life, blinked. Then she laughed and flung up her hands. 'When you put it like that, I can't argue.'

So today Izzy ran in the empty park; revelled in the physical stretching of her capacities; savoured the diamond-bright dew and the lazy heron—and stayed on the alert.

Pepper did not need to warn her about the dangers of men with guns. Izzy had first-hand experience to draw on. Though that, too, was part of her secret. Nobody knew it. Not even Jemima.

Maybe one day I'll tell them, she thought. Pepper and Jemima—even Adam.

But the thought of handsome Adam Sadler made her shake her head. No, it was impossible to tell him. Adam was a banker. He thought the most dangerous thing that could happen was the US economy going into recession. Whereas Izzy knew that danger came at you in combat gear with crazy eyes and—

She swallowed. It all seemed so far away from London and her busy life these days. Sometimes it even felt as if it had happened to someone else—a story she'd read in one of the Sunday magazines. Or as if she had split into two people on that bus on the jungle track. One Izzy had come home and flung herself into the family enterprise and was doing just *fine*.

Only the other Izzy was still lost. And Adam Sadler, with his Lotus and his Rolex and his membership of a ferociously expensive City gym, was not the man to help her find herself. Even if she wanted him to.

Well, she'd better stay lost today, thought Izzy, revving up for the final push. Today there were more important things to think about. Today was going to take a lot of handling. Today was *serious*.

And there were definitely problems on the horizon. Last night Pepper had been showing signs of climbing the walls. And Jemima was jet-lagged out of her brains. But somehow or other they had to pull it all together for the launch. Because today was crunch time.

Izzy flung back her head, the loose red hair flying. 'And the crunch is what I do,' she said firmly. 'Crisis a speciality. The others can freak all they want. I'll bring home the bacon.'

And she lengthened her stride, put her head down, and went through the pain barrier.

When she got back to the apartment Pepper was sitting huddled over the kitchen table surrounded by three cups of barely touched coffee and clutching a sheet of paper covered with sticky notes. She looked up when Izzy came in. But she did not really see her, thought Izzy. Her cousin's eyes were wild.

'"A whole new experience",' she was muttering. '"A whole *new* experience". Hello, Izzy. "A *whole* new shopping experience".'

'Stop it,' said Izzy, taking the sheet of paper away from her. 'We went through all this last night.'

Until two in the morning, actually. The woman could hardly have slept at all.

Pepper's smile was perfunctory. 'But I had this idea in bed…'

'Sleep would have been better,' said Izzy. She took the coffee cups away, too, and threw their congealing contents down the sink.

'No. Listen. The statistics—'

Izzy looked round from the sink in disbelief. 'You aren't going to hit a bunch of fashion journalists with statistics?'

'They're *significant*,' said Pepper earnestly.

Izzy shook her head. 'You're on a caffeine burn,' she said kindly. 'Cogs not engaging. Statistics are strictly for back-up stuff in the press pack. You have to keep your speech short and intriguing.'

'But—'

'I'm going to make you some toast,' announced Izzy. 'And eggs. With warm milk. Or hot chocolate. Or champagne. You will have something to eat and drink that isn't caffeine. And you will please stop gibbering. *Out of the Attic* is a fantastic idea and this launch is going to be awesome. Right?'

Pepper gave her a better smile this time. 'You're very good to me, Izzy. I'm glad I've got a cousin like you.'

Izzy grinned at her. 'Likewise, oh retail genius. Now, go and have your shower while I rout Jemima out of her pit.'

Jemima had swirled the duvet round her like a Swiss roll and was about as welcoming as a grizzly disturbed in its winter quarters.

'Go 'way.'

'Nope.'

'You're a nightmare. Push off, Nightmare.'

Ruthlessly Izzy flung open the curtains. Golden sun blazed in. Jemima screamed and pulled the pillow over her face.

'I hate you,' she said, muffled but passionate. She was clearly a lot more awake than she wanted to be.

'Sure you do,' said Izzy with a grin. 'Get up.'

'I only just got to sleep.'

'Tough. You have work to do.'

Jemima let out a wail. 'Tell me something new.'

'And a cousin to support.'

There was a pause. Then the pillow was pushed aside a fraction. One eye and a lot of tousled hair appeared.

'Izzy?' said Jemima, as she'd used to do when Izzy woke her on school days.

'That's the one,' said Izzy cheerfully. She added cunningly, 'If you get up now, I'll do eggy bread for breakfast.'

There was a moment's complete silence. Then Jemima groaned and heaved the pillow aside. She sat up.

'Okay. It's not a nightmare,' she said, resigned. 'You're here and you won't go away until I do what you want. What do you want?'

Izzy brought a list out of her pocket and handed it to her.

Jemima stared at it, then looked up at her in disbelief. 'You can't be serious.'

'Starting,' said Izzy, preparing to leave, 'with Pepper's make-up. She'll be ready for you in about ten minutes.'

'Oh.' Jemima sagged back among the remaining pillows. 'All right.' Her voice began to slur again. 'I'll be out in ten minutes.'

'Sure you will,' said Izzy sweetly. And took the duvet with her.

She ignored the roar of outrage that followed her into the corridor. And sure enough, heavy-eyed and spitting, Jemima was in the kitchen with full make-up kit and a hugely magnifying mirror inside five minutes. She spurned the eggy bread with dignity, but she swallowed two cups of coffee and then peered at herself in the mirror.

'Eye bags,' she said, like a surgeon giving a diagnosis. She snapped her fingers. 'Ice.'

Izzy got a bag of ice cubes from the freezer and watched, fascinated, as Jemima applied them to her puffy eyes.

'Old model-girl trick,' she said between her teeth. 'Being the face of Belinda has taught me a lot of those.'

She did not sound as if it was a lesson she was entirely happy about. Izzy was whipping eggs for Pepper's breakfast, but at that she looked up sharply. Jemima had not only stopped listening, she realised with a pang, she had stopped confiding, too.

'Everything okay, Jay Jay?'

'Just great. I live in five-star hotels and when I wake up in the morning I don't know which continent I'm in.'

Izzy's eyebrows rose. 'Is that good or bad?'

'It's a living,' said Jemima without expression.

Izzy was beginning to get worried. When Jemima had been selected by cosmetics house Belinda to be the face of their new campaign, all the papers had said this put her in the superstar league. It was the height of every model's ambition, they'd said. But this did not sound like a woman enjoying well-deserved success. This sounded like a woman with problems.

But now was not the time to talk about it.

'Let's go for a pizza this evening, when the razzmatazz is all over,' Izzy said.

Jemima gave a harsh laugh. 'Who has time for pizza? I go straight from the presentation to the airport.'

'You mean you won't even be coming back here to pick up a bag?' Izzy was shocked.

Jemima shook her head.

Izzy was filled with compunction. 'I'm sorry I took the duvet off you this morning.'

'If you hadn't, I'd have slept for a week,' said Jemima. 'You don't want to know how mad my life is.'

But before she could say any more Pepper emerged in a bathrobe. She had another sheaf of printed tables in her hand.

'Jemima, Izzy—what do you think? I could just run through…'

More pressing concerns took over.

'No statistics,' they yelled in unison.

'You,' said the woman from the PR agency, 'are a genius. I didn't think it could be done.' She had spiky, lurid green hair and a clipboard and she was terrifyingly professional.

Izzy was on a roll. She was good at crisis management, and this morning she was getting plenty of opportunity. Now she stopped tacking a piece of chintz across a nook full of wires and looked up. She tucked a stray lock of red hair back under her gypsy headscarf. 'What?'

'Getting the Beast of Belinda here before ten o'clock in the morning. She looks like a dream, all right. But that woman *bites*.'

Izzy was affronted. 'I'm sorry?'

But the clipboard had already zipped to the other side of the big glass-walled reception room.

The in-house cameraman stopped adjusting his focus on the small stage and looked down at Izzy. 'Molly means thank you for keeping Jemima sweet. She hasn't actually sunk her teeth into anyone yet.'

Izzy blinked. 'Beast of Belinda?' she echoed.

He pulled a wry face. 'Jemima Dare. Face of Belinda Cosmetics. Newest of the supermodels. And doesn't she know it!'

And my sister, thought Izzy. Probably not a good moment to mention it, though. Normally she would go to war with her sister's enemies at the drop of a hat. But twelve minutes before they opened the door on the launch of *Out of the Attic* was bad timing by anyone's standards.

She flicked the chintz into expert folds and stapled it in place. 'You know Jemima Dare?' she said with deceptive mildness.

'I've worked with her.'

'Phew, yes,' said the cameraman's assistant, with feeling. 'Serious pain in the ass, that one.'

Izzy held onto her temper with an effort. 'How interesting,' she said between her teeth.

She hammered an errant nail into place with force, flicked a dustsheet over the whole construction and stood up.

'Done?' said the woman with the clipboard, zipping back as if she were on rollerblades. 'Can we let the punters in yet?'

Izzy cast a narrow-eyed look round the big reception room. It did not look like the launch of anything. It looked as if it was in the throes of refurbishment. Pots of paint stood around, amid step ladders and mysterious outcrops of furniture under dust sheets. The pictures on the walls were draped in sheeting and the big central chandelier was at the end of the room, leaning drunkenly against a trestle table. The carpet had gone. The London fashion crowd were in for a shock.

'Yup. Ready to rock.'

The green-haired woman grinned. 'I was right. Genius. Culp and Christopher would be a happy agency if all our clients were practical like you.'

'Practical is what I do,' agreed Izzy.

'Sure is.' The woman consulted her clipboard. 'I've got the girls in position to hand out the goody bags. So we'll open up the moment you give me the sign.'

She powered over to the big doors to the conference hall.

Izzy nodded and checked that her earpiece was in place. Then she pressed the connect button and spoke into her collar mike. 'Testing. Testing. The partygoers are at the gates. Are we ready? Speak to me, people... Tony? Geoff?'

They were there. She ran through the roll call of her other helpers one by one. All in place, raring to go. Then at last she came to her cousin Pepper.

She was not worried about her décor, or the timing of her effects, but she was worried about Pepper. Should you be that nervous before the launch of a ground-breaking new business?

'Pepper? How's it going?'

There was an audible gulp. 'Fine,' quavered Pepper.

Izzy turned to face the wall, so that there was no chance of a passer by hearing her. She switched to one-to-one transmission and said into her mike, very softly, 'Come on Big Shot. Entrepreneurs don't panic. You can do this thing.'

There was a slightly watery chuckle. 'You got evidence of that?'

'You blagged the money men. After that, how hard can a bunch of journalists be?'

'Yes, but—'

'What's more,' interrupted Izzy ruthlessly, 'you convinced me and you convinced Jemima. She knows all about clothes and I hate the things. So there you are. Every sector covered.'

This time the chuckle was a lot more robust. 'So it is. Thanks, Izzy.'

'My pleasure.' She switched back to broadcast. 'Okay, everyone. Showtime!'

She gave the thumbs-up to the woman with the clipboard. The tall doors were flung back. The waiting audience clattered in—and stopped dead at the decorators' disarray.

Izzy could have danced with glee. *Great!* This was a launch they wouldn't forget.

She said into the mike, 'Geoff, city sounds please.'

At once a tape full of combustion engines and sirens and voices filled the room. The audience, London sophisticates to a woman, were even more intrigued. They began to move round the room, looking at the shrouded shapes questioningly.

'Right,' said Izzy. 'Got them. Pepper, you're on. Tony, start the light show now.'

The harsh lighting began to dim and a patch of rosy warmth appeared on the shambolic stage. It was empty. It should not have been empty.

Izzy's heart sank. She must not let it show, though. 'Pepper?' she prompted into her mike, sounding as casual as she could manage.

And a blessed, blessed voice said in her ear, 'We're here, Izzy. We're just going on.'

It was Jemima. It should not have been Jemima. Jemima should have followed Pepper onto the stage for dramatic effect.

Technically, she was only there to model a couple of outfits and mingle with the guests. 'I'll do the robot in the gear,' she had said, right from the start. 'But I haven't got time to learn a script.' Yet here she was, stepping into the breach, just as Izzy would have done in her place.

Huh! Beast of Belinda indeed, thought Izzy, bursting with pride. This was no pain in the ass. This was a fully paid-up member of the Girls Stick Together Club.

She said into the mike, 'Go for it, Jay Jay.'

Jemima walked out onto the platform like a queen. Well, a queen taking a day off to paint the nursery, maybe, thought Izzy ruefully. As they had planned in various transatlantic e-mails, Jemima was wearing paint-stained dungarees. There were flecks of paint and ink over her hands and forearms. And her legendary hair was caught up in a tangly ponytail. The audience stopped chattering to their neighbours and frankly stared.

'Life,' said Jemima, standing close to the sound system and reading Izzy's script from the palm of her hand without anyone noticing, 'is a mess. Too fast. Too dirty. Too many disappointments.' She paused.

'Not,' said a soft husky voice, out of sight, 'always.'

From behind an edifice covered in dustsheets, a large, beautiful woman came out into the middle of the stage. She had a mass of gleaming red hair, she was dressed in a silk coat of peacock colours, and she was smiling. Pepper had come a long way since the sisters had taken her bathrobe and statistics away from her this morning.

It looked as if she had got over her momentary panic, too. *Thank you, Jay Jay.* But still Izzy crossed her fingers, just in case.

The audience gasped. This was not what they were expecting at all. This was no model. This was Pepper Calhoun herself. Entrepreneur, innovator and, just possibly, retail genius.

The light changed again, turned gold. The whole room was bathed in the soft glow of a summer evening. Birds cheeped. Insects buzzed. A stream chattered faintly in the distance. Ripples of light like water began to flicker across the shrouded shapes. Even the nosiest journalist dropped the corner of the dustsheet in simple awe.

'Hi, there,' said Pepper, in her soft American accent.

To Izzy's relief she was as cool and friendly as if she had opened the door to a bunch of friends. Just as Izzy had coached her for a week. She sounded as if she did not have a nerve in her body and had never even heard of retail statistics.

'Good to see you,' she went on. 'Glad you can be here with us today.'

So she was right back on Izzy's carefully crafted script. Cautiously, Izzy uncrossed her fingers. Looking good, she thought. Looking more than good.

Pepper smiled sleepily around the room. She seemed to catch the eye of every single person of that select group there.

That was Izzy's idea, too. They had practised it in the flat, over and over again, until Pepper had been reeling and Izzy had been gloomily certain it would never work. Now she held her breath.

Jemima stretched her arms out in front of her, as if she were easing her shoulders after a hard painting session. Only Izzy noticed that she was turning her hand so she could read from the back of it.

'Couldn't get the show on in time, eh, Pepper?' she said as lightly as if she had only just thought of it. 'What went wrong?'

The glittering green and blue figure on the stage beside her smiled.

'Sometimes,' she said, 'you just have to trust your imagination.'

That was the signal.

'Geoff, Tony, ladies…' murmured Izzy into her mike, more for herself than her well rehearsed team.

'Let your fancy fly,' said Pepper, laughing.

And the lights went out, right on cue.

There was a rush of cool air. Thank God they'd mastered the air-conditioning in time, thought Izzy. Half an hour ago she would not have put money on it.

The tape changed to strange, unearthly music. The darkened ceiling suddenly gleamed with a million stars. There was a concerted gasp from the audience.

Yes! thought Izzy. She let herself breathe again.

There was another gasp as the dustsheets rose like flock of huge birds before flopping to the floor like paper. Silent-footed, the junior helpers folded and rolled the sheets, getting them rapidly out of sight. Izzy waved them away. But they had rehearsed this. They didn't need any more direction. They had all identified their nearest exit. Now they melted through the various doors while the audience was still staring entranced at the starscape.

Izzy was the last to go. She held the door to the kitchen open the tiniest crack so she could see the effect of her production. She was not disappointed. When the lights came up, there was a long indrawn breath of wonder from a hundred throats.

The reception room had magically turned into a big attic, full of sunlight. Wooden trunks of clothes stood invitingly open. Comfortable shabby chairs were set beside old fashioned clothes horses from which every colour of garment hung. There were cushions and books and pot-pourri, and the friendly smell of coffee and fresh bread. The guests looked around, enchanted, as if they could not believe their eyes.

Izzy let the door swing shut. She looked round the stainless steel work surfaces of the empty kitchen as if she didn't quite know how she had got there.

'We did it.' She sounded dazed, even to her own ears.

'You did it,' said Geoff.

They shared a high five.

On the monitoring system they heard Pepper saying serenely, 'Welcome to *Out of the Attic*. A whole new shopping experience.' On the black and white screen above their heads, she spread her hands. 'Enjoy.'

They did. They wandered round as if they had just discovered a treasure chest. Women who lived all their professional lives in designer black threw scarlet and gold shawls around themselves and looked wistfully in the mirror. Hard-bitten fashion professionals ran their hands sensuously over velvet and angora and sighed.

Izzy slid rapidly along to the Ladies' Room to change out of her working decorator gear. Now that the theatrical tricks were over she had to turn herself back into Pepper's efficient assistant and work the room. She was already hauling the dark tee shirt over her head as she walked in.

Jemima was at a basin, scrubbing the ink prompts off her hands. She looked up when the door opened and grinned at Izzy in the mirror.

'That was a blast. Proud of yourself?'

'I suppose I am, quite,' Izzy admitted.

Jemima flicked water at her. 'Make that lots. You've got them eating out of Pepper's hand.'

Izzy wriggled out of her jeans. 'You did your share. What happened up there? Pepper freak out?'

Jemima shrugged. 'Said she couldn't remember her words and you'd told her not to go into detail too early.' She shook her head. 'She may be a retail genius, but she sure doesn't talk the talk.'

'She does with a little help from her friends,' said Izzy. 'You handled that brilliantly.'

She splashed cold water under her arms and the back of her neck.

Jemima watched as she towelled off and pulled on sheer dark tights. 'I couldn't make head or tail of Pepper's gibbering. So I went back to the first speech you wrote and said, ''You do this bit; I'll do that.'''

'Worked like a dream.' Izzy's voice was muffled as she pulled a slim charcoal-grey dress over her head. 'Looked good, too. Very cool. How did you get her to do it?'

'I told her she owed you.' Jemima was whipping her maltreated hair into place with expert rapidity.

'*Owed* me?'

'Yup.'

'Owed *me*? But this is her project, her idea. I wouldn't even have a job if it weren't for Pepper and *Out of the Attic*.'

'Correction. You'd have another job.'

'Maybe. But—'

'No maybe about it,' broke in Jemima. She stopped fiddling with her hair and sent Izzy a minatory look. 'Don't put yourself down. You can turn your hand to anything.'

'So can the odd job man in our block.'

Jemima ignored that. 'And you're always the best, too.'

Izzy smiled in spite of herself. 'You're prejudiced.' She cast a cursory look in the mirror and fluffed her hair out.

'Let me do that,' said Jemima impatiently.

She pressed Izzy into one of the small gilt chairs and took up a brush. Her own tangled ponytail had been an artful creation, whereas Izzy's tangles were the result of too little attention and a hectic three hours spent scrambling among the installations.

'I am going to give you a present of a day at a decent salon,' Jemima said, attacking the tangles ruthlessly. 'When did you last have your hair done properly?'

Izzy chuckled. 'The last time you gave me a present of a day at a salon.'

Jemima smacked her lightly with the brush. 'How you have the gall to lecture Pepper, I'll never know.'

'That's different. That's business. It matters how Pepper looks.'

'It matters how everyone looks,' said Jemima, shocked to the core.

'Believe me, it doesn't.'

Jemima paused in her work. She met her sister's eyes in the mirror.

'You mean when you were hiking round the world you had more important things to think about than your split ends?' she interpreted.

Izzy was shocked. 'Am I that smug?'

'You're that weird,' corrected Jemima. She extracted the last tangle and pursed her lips. 'Plait,' she decided. 'No option. Don't fidget, I gotta concentrate.'

'I'm not weird,' said Izzy, offended.

'Yes, you are. Don't give me that nonsense about not caring about clothes. You love clothes. But you're always finding stuff for other people. I used to think it was just me. But since Pepper arrived you're always coming home with things to suit her, too. Never you.'

Izzy shrugged. 'Well, you two are on display all the time. I'm a backroom girl.'

Jemima was whipping threads of thick red hair into a plait. They kept springing free.

'Oh, this is hopeless. I need gel. Don't move.' She rootled through her bag, saying over her shoulder, 'You go to parties. Most people like to look good at a party.'

Izzy clicked her tongue. 'I go to parties to meet people. Not to be looked at.'

'Thank you,' said Jemima dryly.

Izzy slewed round. 'I didn't mean—'

'Don't *move*.' Jemima found the gel. 'And, yes, you did mean it,' she said. 'And I'm tired of it. At some point you decided that I was the pretty one. So you delegated caring about clothes and makeup and stuff to me. Boring.'

'I—'

But Jemima was combing the gel through her hair with busy fingers and refused to be interrupted.

'You're not on some broken-down Latin American bus any more. You live in London. You have a job. *Out of the Attic* sells clothes, for heaven's sake. Wake up and start looking in the mirror. You're beautiful.'

This time the hair slid sweetly into its elaborate plait.

'There!' Jemima stepped back. 'Bit darker than we started off with, but not bad. Not bad at all.'

Izzy looked at herself. Her hair was still ordinary red. Not Jemima's lustrous firelight tones, not Pepper's curling Titian—plain, common or garden, brickdust-red. But the plait and the fashionable gel made her look alert and faintly dangerous—and at least she was dark auburn for the moment. She grinned.

'Well done.'

'Not finished.'

Before Izzy could complain, Jemima was waving pots and brushes around. They had done this since they were small. Izzy sat very still, resigned.

'Apes groom each other, too, you know,' she said chattily.

'Shut up.' Jemima's eyes narrowed to slits. Then she swooped, lipliner in hand.

It took less than two minutes. Jemima, after all, was a professional model. When she straightened, Izzy had cheekbones. She looked at herself in the mirror, half-bemused, half-uneasy.

'Thank you,' she said, trying to feel grateful.

'Make-up lessons,' said Jemima, committing it to memory. And, with apparent irrelevance, 'You taking Adam to the party, then?'

'No.'

Jemima nodded. She did not look surprised. 'Another one falls at the Third Date fence,' she said sadly. 'What is it with you?'

Izzy knew how to deal with a nosy younger sister. 'The party is work. You know we don't mix work and play.'

'You play?' said Jemima, mock incredulous.

'Watch it, brat!'

'Social skills course *and* make-up lessons,' said Jemima, grinning.

Izzy stood up and gave Jemima a quick hug. 'Don't waste your money,' she advised.

Jemima bit her lip.

'Don't worry about it. I prefer being the sister who bites.'

'I don't care about that,' Jemima said impatiently. 'It's this giving up on clothes and third dates that worries me.'

Izzy grinned. 'I'm just not the pretty one. Get used to it.'

Jemima was packing away her stuff. She glared.

'You're crazy. You ought to be gorgeous. You're three times as much fun as I am. You dance like a maniac. Guys line up and half the time you don't even *see* them. And you look as if you don't own a mirror. And,' yelled Jemima, suddenly losing it, 'I feel—as if—it's my *fault*.'

'Hey. Calm down.' Izzy was disconcerted and a bit annoyed. 'It's nothing to do with you if I look like a rag bag.'

Jemima stopped yelling. But under the exquisite make up her face was drawn and her eyes tired. 'Yes, it bloody is,' she said. 'And we both know it.'

Their eyes met. For a moment there was silence in the luxurious cloakroom. Then Jemima gave a quick, spiky shrug and started to stuff all her tubes and pots and brushes back into the designer tote bag.

'Oh, what's the point?' she said wearily. 'Come on. We've got a cousin's business to promote.'

She stuffed the bag under the coat rack and went back to the conference room without a backward look.

Izzy followed more slowly. There was a faint frown between her brows. It was not like her sister to fly off the handle. Maybe all the time-zone hopping was getting to her.

'You and I,' she muttered, 'have got to have a long talk. And soon.'

But Jemima did not hear. Or did not want to hear. And once in the conference room, like the professional she was, Jemima went instantly into posing beautifully for assorted photographers, her usual vibrant self again.

She had changed into what Pepper hoped would be the *Attic*'s signature outfit: soft full trousers and a shirt with sleeves that an eighteenth-century duellist would have killed for. Jemima's chosen colours were chocolate and amber. They made the glorious hair look alive, as if it had caught lamplight and fire in its depths.

Even Izzy, used to her sister's beauty, was startled.

'She really is gorgeous, isn't she?' she said, almost to herself.

The clipboard queen was passing. 'Gorgeous,' she said indifferently. She stuffed the board under her arm and held out a hand. 'Molly di Peretti from Culp and Christopher. Too much of a rush to do introductions earlier. But I wanted to say how much I admire what you did here today.'

'Thank you,' said Izzy, but absently. She was still looking at Jemima. That outburst was so out of character! What was going on behind the professionally flirtatious manner?

But Molly di Peretti was more interested in the concept of the launch. 'This is just so original. You know, when Pepper told me what you were planning, I told her it was too weird?'

'Oh?' From a distance she could see that Jemima was clearly on edge. Her hands were never still and she kept touching her face, her hair.

'"The hacks want champagne and lots of it," I said. "Coffee and chat won't cut the mustard." That was your idea, right?'

'Yes,' said Izzy absently.

Jemima wasn't happy. Other people might not notice, but Izzy had protected her from her first day in the playground. She could see that, however much her sister smiled, she was just desperate to get away.

'Well, I was wrong,' said Molly, oblivious. 'It's brilliant. Everyone is going to remember this launch.'

Izzy pulled herself together. 'That's the name of the game,' she said gaily.

'Hmm. Not everyone can do it, though.' Molly di Peretti thought a bit. 'And you're Pepper Calhoun's assistant, right? You don't organise events for a living?'

'Good grief, no. I'm just the gofer.'

'Hmm,' she said again. 'And how did you get together with Pepper?'

'We're cousins.'

The woman's eyebrows climbed towards her green hairline. She looked across the room to where Jemima was laughing a little too loudly at something one of the photographers had said. 'Ah. So you must be related to the gorgeous Jemima as well?'

'She's my sister.' Izzy's voice was neutral. She waited for Molly di Peretti to remember that she had called Jemima the Beast of Belinda. She was not vindictive but she would enjoy seeing the brisk sophisticate wince.

But Molly di Peretti was not wincing. She was looking intrigued. 'Lots of talent in your family.' She put her head on one side. 'We might just be able to use that.'

Izzy was trying to gauge how the launch party was going, but at that she stopped looking round the room for a moment and paid attention.

'Use it? How?'

'Woman power,' said Molly, clearly writing the press release in her head. *'Siblings unite to give the fashion establishment a run for its money. Redheads Rule!* There's lots of possibilities.'

Izzy snorted. 'Oh, yeah? And what are you going to call it? *The Brains, the Beauty and the Other One*?' she said with sudden savagery.

Molly flung up a hand in mock surrender. 'Hey. No sweat. It was just an idea.'

Izzy was taken aback by her own vehemence. She said in a calmer voice, 'Sorry. It's just not my scene.'

'Yeah. I can see that,' Molly said slowly.

'Anyway, why would you want to start another story? Isn't this one going to be big enough? Especially with the party tonight?'

'Yup. I wanted to talk to you about that. I may have another guest.'

'Fine.' Izzy shrugged. 'I'll put her on the list. Name?'

Molly rested her chin on her clipboard. 'Dominic Templeton-Burke,' she said. And waited for a reaction.

She did not get one. 'Sounds like another chin-less wonder,' said Izzy, making a note. 'Hope he's pretty.'

Molly's lips twitched. 'Oh, he is. In fact—'

'Great. Now, tell me that you were joking about the three-woman line-up and I'll be a happy bunny.'

Molly hesitated. 'PR is more than one splash, you know. After the launch we'll keep on drip-drip-dripping away. We have to place a story here, a photograph there.'

'But the story doesn't have to be woman power, does it?' said Izzy with foreboding.

'Not if you don't want, of course.' Molly di Peretti did not try to hide her disappointment. 'But that's the message Pepper keeps pounding out.' She sighed. 'In fact, I'd better go circulate among the hacks. Make sure it's getting through.'

She moved on with a friendly smile.

Izzy watched her go. She could have kicked herself. *Not* well handled. Maybe I'm losing my touch with a crisis, she told herself, trying to make a joke of it.

Oh, well, back to work. Check with the boss, check with the team, keep the wheels rolling. If she could find any of them in the suddenly active crowd, of course.

But actually it was easy. The crowd was thickest round her cousin, and they were all listening with attention. Some were even scribbling.

Pepper was on a roll. She might freeze with nerves on a stage, but in a small group, on her own subject, she was unstoppable.

'These are real clothes for real women,' she was saying earnestly. 'We've got some wonderful designers working for us. No more tarty tat for stick insects or black, black, black. *Out of the Attic* is going to be a fun place to come. And you take the fun home with you when you buy one of our outfits.' She twirled the jade and turquoise skirts of her silk coat with manifest delight.

At least one journalist beamed in sympathy. Someone took a photograph.

Izzy bit back a smile. Only this morning in the car coming here, she had said, 'Don't put that in the speech. Keep it for the one-to-one chats. It will make a great quote.'

Pepper met her eyes across the group in a conspiratorial grin. 'Isn't that right, Izzy?'

'Take home the fun? Works for me,' agreed Izzy easily.

The journalists turned. They clocked that she was a member of staff. At once, Izzy saw, they bypassed her face, looking straight at the dress. She would have to get used to that, she thought wryly.

'One of the new designs?' someone asked.

Fluently, Izzy gave them name, designer and catalogue number. They wrote that down, too.

'Let me show you the campaign trunk,' Izzy said, leading them to one of the clusters of furniture. 'We really love this. We found the original in a junk shop and had it copied. See those drawers? That's where we keep accessories. We want the customers to discover them, like secrets.'

The journalists started to pull out the drawers, exclaiming with pleasure at the lavender bags and delicate twisty belts they found there.

'How am I doing?' Izzy said out of the corner of her mouth to Pepper.

'Born saleswoman,' returned Pepper, with a wink. 'Keep on working the room. We're flying!'

She was right. To a woman, the guests loved the idea of a store that invited customers to discover stuff in an attic. Some of them weren't quite so sure about all the clothes themselves. But absolutely everyone loved Jemima's golden shirt. And nobody said a word about the absence of champagne.

Izzy circulated conscientiously for an hour.

'Have you had one of these smoked salmon things?' Pepper asked, nibbling a canapé. 'Boy, I needed that.'

Izzy shook her head. 'Can't risk it. I'll mark the dress. Always been a messy feeder. We'll have pizza later.'

Pepper laughed and let her go. Izzy went to check on her helpers. They had to be ready to clear the room the moment the last guest left. The hotel was on a tight timetable.

'They're having too much fun,' said Geoff, munching on a Bath bun and peering in through the service doors. He offered her a bite.

Izzy shook her head. 'I'll get them out,' she said with confidence.

'How?'

'If they want to go to the nightclub reception this evening, they have to pick up a ticket. From the table in the foyer. All I have to do is go in there and murmur in a few ears and there'll be a stampede.'

He was amused. 'You're good at this, aren't you?'

'I seem to be,' Izzy agreed, after a moment. She sounded surprised.

'That's not all you're good at,' he said, licking the sugar off the top of his bun. 'That was a real *coup de theatre* you got going with the lights and the stars and all. You ever want to work in the theatre, you give me a call.'

She was embarrassed. 'Oh, this was just a one-off. I wasn't even sure it would work.'

'It worked,' he said without emphasis. 'You're a natural. You've got my number. Call me. Maybe next time I'll be employing you, rather than the other way round. Oh, well, action stations.'

He finished his bun, gave her a friendly punch in the shoulder and went to round up his team.

Izzy went back to start the whispering campaign. It cleared the room. In ten minutes the only people who had not moved were Jemima and the woman from the PR company. Izzy waved in her team to start the dismantling operation and still they stayed locked in serious conversation. She sighed and went over to them.

'...off my back,' Jemima was saying with heat.

'But you *can* do it. Today proves that.' Molly di Peretti sounded impatient.

'Today was family.'

'Is that what you want? Are you saying that we have to take your sister onto the pay roll for you to honour your obligations?'

'My sister wouldn't look at you,' flashed Jemima. 'She's got a great job.'

'Then what will it take?'

'Just get off my back.' It was a wail.

Molly said crisply, 'Jemima, no one else will tell you the truth, but I will. You're walking a tightrope. Go on like this and you'll fall off. Nobody's indispensable.'

Hey! thought Izzy. She increased her pace. 'Sorry to break this up, guys. But we have to be out of here in twenty minutes flat. Can you transfer your chat to the bar?'

She put a protective arm round her sister's shoulders. They were as rigid as iron.

Jemima looked round. Her face was hard. She did not look as if she needed anyone's protection.

'Chat over,' she said curtly.

Molly di Peretti shrugged. 'I'll see you in ten days then. If you make it, of course.'

Jemima's expression darkened. 'I'll make it.'

Molly nodded. 'I'll go and round up the spare press packs.'

She went. Jemima glared after her.

'What was that about?' asked Izzy, gathering up some silky tops that had got scattered and bundling them into an open chest.

'Nothing.' Jemima folded a couple of scarves and slapped them down on top of the nearest cabin trunk. 'I *hate* PR,' she burst out. 'Of all the pointless things. They make you do stuff you hate. And you've got to pretend it's all terrific fun all the time. It's worse than gym at bloody school.'

Izzy was startled. 'Jemima—' she began in concern.

But one of the boys was coming over with one of the tea trays on wheels that served as removal trolleys and they had to help him load the furniture.

'We'll talk about the principles of public relations later,' Izzy promised.

Jemima gave a laugh that sounded more like a shriek. 'One day when all this is over,' she agreed.

But then the car was at the door to take her to the airport and there was no time to talk. 'I'll call you,' she said, giving Izzy a swift, hard hug.

It stayed with her all the rest of the day. It had felt like desperation.

'I hope she's all right,' said Izzy, almost to herself.

'She's fine,' said Pepper, overhearing. 'She's the face of Belinda. She's got a diary full of top jobs. And she's through adolescent spots. What can go wrong?'

Izzy could not put her finger on it. 'I—just have a feeling…'

'Quit worrying,' said Pepper, not without sympathy. 'Okay, you've known her since she was minus nine months. But she's all grown-up now, and she knows what she wants. Heck, it's success that most people only dream about. She's feeling great.'

Izzy thought of the conversation she had overheard. 'I'm not sure that's true.'

'I am.'

A lifetime of being the heir to a multi-million-dollar retail empire had given Pepper total confidence in her judgement, Izzy thought. Not a shimmer of doubt there.

She said slowly, 'But this success is very big, very sudden. I'm not sure Jemima really knows how to deal with it.'

'Then she'll learn.' Pepper was impatient. 'I did. You did. You're the most together woman I know. You can deal with anything.' She laughed suddenly. 'In fact, if anyone did try to attack you in the park, I just bet you'd talk him right out of it. No contest.' And she went back to work.

Caught unawares, Izzy felt her head go back as if her cousin had hit her. It was the first time in ages, and it took her right back to two years ago and a small border town in the Andes. Shaken, she watched Pepper walk away.

If only you knew, she thought. *If only you knew.*

CHAPTER TWO

DOMINIC TEMPLETON-BURKE was sitting in the oak-panelled library of the Explorers' Reading Room when his cellphone gave a discreet cough. It was so discreet it was almost inaudible, in fact. Even so, three assorted explorers looked up and glared.

'Sorry,' Dom mouthed.

He went out into the corridor. Tall windows looked down onto a rustic garden, incongruous in the centre of London. He settled himself into a window seat and put the phone to his ear. Below him, late roses were golden in the September sun.

'Yes, Jay?'

'My staff tell me you were perfectly bloody.' Jay Christopher sounded mildly amused.

Dom shifted uncomfortably. Jay was an old friend. 'Not my scene,' he said excusingly.

Jay was unsurprised. 'I warned you. Why don't you just take the book deal? That would sort out all the funding problems at a shot.'

'I keep telling you. I'm a doer, not a writer.'

Jay sighed. 'Okay. Well, Molly has got an idea.'

'What sort of idea?' said Dom suspiciously.

'Oh, some celebrity bash she thinks you should go to. It will get plenty of coverage. Not inspired. But it's a start. She'll call you. Do what she says, Dom,' he ended warningly. 'She knows what's she's doing.'

Molly had obviously been waiting for Jay to finish the softening up process. She rang as soon as he'd put the phone down.

'Hi, Dom. Party tonight. The Flamingo Pool,' she said briskly. 'Wear something tasty.'

Dom blinked. 'Tasty?'

'Something that will get you noticed. We need those photographs in the papers tomorrow.'

Dominic could not resist it. 'You mean like a parka and goggles and no knickers?'

Molly choked on a laugh in spite of herself. 'You can be a real pain in the ass,' she informed him. 'But you're worth it for the cabaret. Go and rent yourself some designer togs and have a session on the sunbed. We're talking serious crumpet for the thinking woman, here.'

Dominic's heart sank. 'Whose party?' he said gloomily.

'Pepper Calhoun. For her new business. Basically the fashion crowd,' said Molly hardily. 'I know it's not your scene, but tough. Where there are frocks there are photographers. Where there are photographers there are celebrities. And where there are celebrities there are columnists. Write yourself two appealing sentences, learn them off by heart, then say them to everyone you meet.'

'Sounds like a fun evening.'

'Who said anything about fun? I thought this was your work!'

Dominic laughed and capitulated. 'You've got me there,' he said ruefully. 'Okay. Tell me where to go and I'll do the pretty.'

Molly gave him the club address. 'Don't get there before eleven-thirty,' she said briskly. 'And polish up your biceps for the cameras. Gotta go. See you tonight.'

Dom went back to the library and submerged himself in the saving sanity of ice drift.

'Somewhere I lost about three hours today,' Izzy said, unpacking boxes from the back of the taxi while Molly di Peretti rang the bell in the Flamingo Pool's ominously dark entrance. 'We were supposed to go out for pizza. But then it took longer to clear up than I expected.

'Publicity parties always take longer than you expect,' said Molly absently. The intercom asked a question and she leant towards it. 'Hi, Franco, it's me. We've brought the stuff for the *Out of the Attic* party.'

'Then Pepper put in an extra meeting,' said Izzy, struggling with a couple of banners that, even folded, were as big as she was. 'And Jemima booked me into her hairdresser's. Somehow lunch just got lost.'

The door swung open by remote control. Molly propped it open with her briefcase and came back to the taxi to help unload. Together she and Izzy carried boxes of balloons, decorations and party favours into the building.

'Leave them there,' said Molly with authority. 'Josh can carry them upstairs and put them up. That's what new recruits are for. You and I are management.'

'Huh. Management doesn't eat, apparently.'

'Proves we're serious,' said Molly hardily. 'And we're running the coolest party of the season to prove it.'

Izzy followed her up the stairs and onto the main dance floor. She stopped dead.

'This is cool?' she said incredulously.

Izzy liked to dance, and she went to a lot of clubs. She was used to a driving beat and searing spotlights that blinked through the feverish dark. It was vibrant, exciting, *dangerous*. But the room she had entered was just depressing. In the light of a hundred-watt bulb, the floor was stained, the mirrors smeared and the bar had bits gouged out of it.

'Are you sure?'

Molly di Peretti chuckled. 'This is what they all look like when the lights are on. The imagination doesn't get going until the lights go down. It's going to be great. A real party to remember. Trust me.'

She was right, too. It was the same basic crowd as the morning. But this evening the women brought their partners. And Culp and Christopher's list of celebrity guests had all turned up, agog. The clothes were stylish; the music was *hot*.

Pepper, who did not normally go clubbing, began to look punch drunk by eleven o'clock. Her Steven, steady as a rock, put an arm round her.

'How long do you have to stay, my love?'

Pepper leaned gratefully into his shoulder but said, 'It's my party. I'll stick it out to the end.'

He looked down at her tenderly. 'Sure? No one would notice if I carried you off right now. Would they, Izzy?'

Izzy looked away. Steven Konig was not her type, but there was something about the warmth in his eyes when he looked at her cousin that made her almost—well, sad. *Grow up,* she told herself. *You're the one who keeps passing on the third date. Your choice.*

Aloud she said, ''Course they wouldn't. Anyway, you won't get me out of here till dawn. If you want someone from *Out of the Attic* to hand out the balloons and turn off the lights, I'll do it.'

Steven smiled at her gratefully. And it was quite, quite different from the way he looked at Pepper. Just as well, thought Izzy, ignoring the little pain round her heart. She tossed her hair and boogied to the beat. 'Take her home, Steven. And don't wait up. This is my element. I was born to dance.'

She flung herself back on the dance floor and set out to prove it.

Izzy did not remember that she was running on her emergency tank. The combined effects of too many late nights and thirty hours without solid food gave her a pleasant sense of flying. There was no deadline, no last-minute hitches to sort out, no speeches to write. Above all, there was no man pressing her to respond to something she knew in her bones was not what she wanted.

She was wearing *Out of the Attic*'s Christmas party number. Bright red, lots of skirt, most of it slashed to hip height and a boned top that left her shoulders bare and her cleavage spectacular.

Jemima's hairstylist had got rid of her gelled *queue*, and now feathery red hair tumbled seductively about her bare shoulders. Izzy threw out her arms and let the music take her.

Or so it seemed to Dominic Templeton-Burke, walking in alone at midnight.

He stopped dead. 'Who—is—*that*?' he said with deep appreciation.

Molly di Peretti had been called to sign him in. She looked at the wild thing in scarlet on the dance floor and grinned. 'That's management. Or a woman with hidden depths, depending on your point of view.'

Dominic took an enthusiastic step forward.

'My point of view is altogether too far away from the hottest babe in the place. Lead me to her.'

Molly barred his path. 'Hey. Let's not forget what we're doing here. This is supposed to be work.'

Dom did not take his eyes off the supple whip-fast dancer. His lips twitched. 'I'll give it my best shot,' he assured Molly. He swung past her with a neat evasive movement.

She blocked him even more neatly. 'Focus, Dominic. Focus! The point of tonight is to get you off the science pages and into the gossip columns.'

The dancer raised her arms above her head. Her head fell back, eyes shut, lips parted. She was utterly surrendered to the music. Dom drew a soundless breath.

'Done,' he said, putting Molly out of his way with one decisive movement.

But she was a tryer. She hung onto his arm. 'The woman you've got your greedy eye on has absolutely no publicity profile at all. There's no point in you dancing with her.'

Dom smiled.

'Well, no professional point,' Molly amended. She snorted. 'Look, there's only one place dancing like that will get you, and it isn't into tomorrow's newspapers. You do realise that?'

Dom's smile widened wickedly. But his eyes did not waver. He was not looking at Molly. 'I'm counting on it.'

Molly let him go and flung up her hands. 'Okay. Waste your best chance. See if I care.'

But she could see that it did not matter what she said. He was already moving purposefully into the dancing crowd. She did not think he'd even heard her.

'Grrrr,' she said. Then shrugged. She'd just have to tell Abby that she had done her best and Dom wouldn't co-operate. Somehow she did not think Abby would be surprised.

*　　*　　*

Dom had never seen anyone so completely absorbed. He homed in on the wild haired dancer with the unstoppable force of an arrow, brushing other people aside like falling leaves. They fell back, amused, seeing where he was headed. Not much doubt about his object; everyone could see that. Dancers parted obligingly, as he shouldered his way through the crowd.

In the end it seemed that there was only one person who did not know where he was headed. Eyes tight shut, his lady in red was in her own world, letting her hips do the talking.

Eloquently, thought Dominic. His breath quickened.

She was like a fantasy creature. Concentrated. Intense. Passionate.

In the flickering light, droplets seemed to gleam on the skin between her breasts. Condensation from the air conditioning? Some sparkly cosmetic? Sweat? Whatever it was, she was oblivious. Dom wanted to lick it off and find out.

The heat of desire hit him in the throat. For a moment he could hardly breathe. And *still* she didn't notice.

He reached her. He put a hand on her swaying hip. It was very gentle, but—and with a shock Dom realised it—it said, *Mine*.

The woman's eyes flew open as if he had bounced her out of a deep sleep. Her hips did not stop moving to the beat but for a second her feet tangled themselves up. She faltered, almost losing the rhythm.

Before she could stagger Dom put his other round her waist and braced her, his open palm along her spine. Her back was naked.

Her eyes widened but the music had her in thrall. She did not stop moving. He matched his hip movements to hers.

'You are amazing,' he said. Well, he mouthed it at her. Not much hope of her hearing him over the thunderous guitars. 'I want some.'

Some? All! But he could take that up later.

She shook her head. But he could not tell if that was a rejection or she just couldn't hear him.

He hesitated. Then thought, She's not dancing as if she's rejecting me.

Dom moved in closer. And closer. Their hips touched.

The woman did not pull away. Oh, she swayed back, of course. But when the music told her to she swayed forward, too. Her breasts brushed across his chest—deliberately? Or was it by chance? No more than an accidental touch, caused by her abandonment to the music? Did she even *see* him?

Dom groaned, unheard. And then realised their eyes were locked. Something told him she was seeing the moment of intense sensation in his face. Something made her eyes gleam anyway. Amusement? Sheer female triumph? Lust?

He felt sweat break out along the back of his neck. *If it isn't lust, I'm in deep trouble.*

The track finished. For a moment she seemed to hang suspended, not unmoving exactly, but like a butterfly, beating the air with its wings while it hesitates between one direction and the next. He put a hand on her hip. No doubt about this one. Totally deliberate.

She looked startled.

And then, with a crash, the air was full of a salsa beat, fast and sexy. She plunged into a spiky routine and Dom did something he had never done before. He pulled her into his arms almost roughly, slid his thigh between hers, and took control.

She seemed to shimmer in his hands. Not with resistance, but as if for a moment she did not know what was happening. Then, in a second, he felt her total surrender.

Yes!

Her body moulded itself against him, as if they had danced like this a thousand times before. And

they went into a routine that he had not even realised he knew.

It was like a cycle of the universe. Urgent, fast,
yet still somehow unhurried. Tense, exciting, but
underneath they both knew they were on a
straight road and journey's end was inevitable.

It was like making love.

The music changed. Dom bent his tall head,
brushed her soft hair away and put his lips to her
ear.

'Time we were somewhere else.'

He felt her hesitate for the tiniest moment. He
could not bear it. His hands tightened in spite of
himself.

'*Please,*' he said in a ragged voice. He could
not ever remember saying please like that before.
It shocked him for a moment.

But then she shook back her head and gave him
the most wonderful smile, and he forgot everything except that they had to be alone. *Now.*

'Get your coat,' he said curtly.

Her eyes widened. She looked almost dazed.

'No coat?'

She swallowed. Shook her head.

'Then let's go.'

He put a hand under her bare elbow and turned
her towards the door. She did not resist but she

was quivering. Well, hell, what was surprising about that? So was he.

They were like machines that had just been turned on. Engines thrumming. Idling, but under power. *Ready.*

He wanted her so badly it hurt. And she wanted him. No doubt about that. She was not looking anywhere but at him, and the pulse in her throat throbbed to the same beat as his own.

Dom gave a laugh that was half a groan.

'Shawl? Bag?'

She did not answer. But there was a tiny bag in the same scarlet material as her dress on the bar. Dom swept it up as they passed.

On the stairs, her trembling increased. She clung to him.

'You should have brought a coat,' scolded Dom, teasing.

But he paused to shrug off his jacket and tuck it round her shoulders. As the silk lining slid over her shoulders she gave a voluptuous shiver. Their bodies were so close that he felt it run through from hip to heart.

'Don't *do* that,' he murmured, in mock despair. 'Not yet anyway.'

She gave a little excited laugh, and leaned closer.

'Yes,' he agreed to that silent demand. 'Home. Now.'

He pushed open the outer door into the September night. She swayed.

'Imagination,' she said.

Late arrivals were getting out of a taxi. Dom commandeered it. He looked over his shoulder. 'What?'

'Imagination doesn't get going until the lights go down.'

He turned to face her. 'A philosopher,' he said, his eyes full of tender amusement. 'You're wrong, though. My imagination got going the moment I walked into that place and saw you.' He held out a hand. 'Come with me?'

She stopped swaying.

'Yes,' she said.

It was not until later—a lot later, when Dom was asking himself what on earth had happened—that he remembered. She had sounded surprised.

CHAPTER THREE

Izzy was having a wonderful dream. A man was taking her into his arms and she wanted him to. She kissed him harder and longer than he kissed her. They belonged.

She did not know his name. She did not think they had even met before. Certainly not in the real world. But they had known each other before time began. She knew that as she knew her own name. And that she was in paradise.

When she needed to take a breath, at last, she lifted her head. 'The best sort of dream,' she gasped.

She felt his chest lift with laughter.

'Like I said, a philosopher.'

She couldn't quite make out his face. But that was dreams for you. They gave you what you wanted in your deepest, deepest soul. But they didn't necessarily let you see all the signposts along the way.

And who needed to see anything when his mouth was sending such wonderful sensations through her skin?

And his voice! He had a voice like dark chocolate. Delicious and totally sinful.

'Say something else,' she demanded.

He was placing soft, playful kisses along her
collarbone. At that he raised his head. 'You want
to *talk*?'

The wonderful sensation began to ebb away.

'Don't stop,' moaned Izzy.

'Well, I wasn't going to.'

The dark chocolate voice was warm, spiced
with laughter. Like a fire on a cold night. A cold
and lonely night. She snuggled against the voice
and felt her head spin pleasantly.

'But you were the one who wanted to talk,' he
pointed out. 'So—we'll talk.' He feathered a kiss
between her breasts. 'Or not talk. Choose!'

Izzy gave a little voluptuous shiver. 'This is *my*
dream,' she said reproachfully. 'I don't wanna
choose. Shouldn't have to. In your own dream,
you're supposed to have it all.'

'All it is, then,' he said against her skin. 'What
do you want to talk about?'

She frowned. 'Not me. You. I want you to tell
me wonders.'

'Wonders?' He sounded startled. She felt his
warm breath on her bare skin.

Izzy stretched her arms above her head and
gave a sigh of total bliss.

'Mmm. Persuade me with promises. Seduce me with a sonnet.' Was it her imagination, or was she slurring her words?

'A *sonnet*?'

Izzy opened her eyes. She seemed to be in spacecraft, hurtling forward among strange planets. Too many lights flashing past, decided Izzy. So she half shut her eyes again and concentrated on the important things.

'I want to be wooed,' she announced dreamily. 'Tell me I'm beautiful.'

'Now, that I can do.'

Her dream lover had wrapped her in his ceremonial robe—which left him with just a thin shirt between her and his alien warmth. She drew a long, luxurious breath, savouring the scent of unknown skin and the whole new world he came from. He had something on his wrist, all dials and lights—probably an interplanetary homing device.

'Do you think I read too much science fiction?' Izzy wondered aloud.

His arm tightened. 'I think you're wonderful, whether you read poetry, science fiction or gardening catalogues,' he told her with feeling.

'Mmmm.' She rubbed her face against his wrist. It felt hot as fire and smelled of sandalwood. She closed her eyes and listened to his pulse. It felt like her own.

The silver spacecraft seemed to go faster. Then braked to a hovering stop.

Her alien said, 'We would be more comfortable inside, don't you think?'

There was a cool rush of air. The vehicle burned off into the universe, leaving Izzy in the arms of her cavalier. In the sudden silence there was faint ringing in her ears. Her head was now definitely dancing, as if she was on a merry-go-round.

From a long way away, he seemed to say, 'Let's get you indoors. Then we can discuss your wooing programme.'

The merry-go-round seemed to speed up. Right out of control, in fact.

Izzy leaned into him. He felt like a rock. How could he not be dizzy, too, when the whole world was spinning faster and faster? The man must be made of iron, she thought. It mildly annoyed her. She was used to being the one with the iron grip on reality.

'This,' she said very carefully, 'is a new experience. A—wholly—new—experience.'

And flopped in his arms, limp as a rag doll.

The last thing she remembered was her alien saying ruefully, 'I should have seen this coming.

It's all right, sweetheart. Hang onto me. I've got you safe.'

'Safe,' she said, not slurring the word at all.

And passed out cold.

She woke up feeling strange. Her mouth was dry, her ribs ached as if she had been kicked—and the window was in the wrong place. The window—!

Izzy sat bolt upright. Her heart thumped like a metronome.

But the window was not an empty space between rotting timbers, with palm trees rattling and creaking outside. It had glass. And curtains. As her eyes adjusted, she saw that she was in a strange bedroom.

Well—bedroom! It was more like an office with mattress space. There was a desk with a huge flat computer screen. Maps and charts all but covered the walls. There was one wall of CDs and another of videos and DVDs. A bookcase brimmed over with books and papers and photographs. A fraying rug in gorgeous colours sat in the middle of the stripped oak floor.

No, this was definitely no Andean rebel hide-out.

Izzy put a hand to her breast. Slowly her breathing came back under control. That was when she recognised the pain under her ribs, too. Hunger!

Hunger? Why on earth was she hungry? What time was it? She looked at her watch. It was four in the morning.

That was when she simultaneously realised three things: she was still wearing the flimsy red Christmas dress that she had put on for *Out of the Attic*'s party; she had left the party with a fantasy figure whose face she could not remember; she had not the foggiest idea where she was.

'Oops,' said Izzy.

She swung her legs out of bed. Well, at least she was alone. No fantasy figure was sleeping heavily on the pillow beside her.

Izzy did not know whether she was disappointed or relieved. On the whole, relieved, she decided. But she could not help wondering who the man was. Had she just latched onto him last night as he was leaving the party? It seemed horribly possible. After all, complete strangers didn't kiss each other passionately in the back of London taxi cabs.

No, decided Izzy, those kisses—and her even more embarrassing demand to be seduced with poetry—had to be a dream. Sleeplessness and starvation had obviously combined to knock her out, and some kind person must have brought her here to recuperate. The mysterious stranger with his fiery kisses had been straight out of a dream. Whoever had brought her to this strange house, it could not be a fantasy hero. Not possibly.

'I hope,' she muttered.

She pattered softly round the room. It looked as if someone had made up a bed for her but had balked at taking her clothes off. Not that there was that much to take off, she thought ruefully. She found her shoes, the charmingly impractical matching bag that Pepper had given her—and somebody's jacket.

She picked it up. And dropped it immediately. It might have been red-hot, she let it go so fast.

Oh, Lord, she knew that smell. It was imprinted on her memory. In part it was her own—her perfume, her shampoo, the new, fresh smell of tonight's silk dress—and in part it was his. *His!*

Izzy swallowed. In the dark she could feel her cheeks burning.

'Time to go,' she told herself sturdily.

The handbag was so tiny there was no room for anything in it—not even her slim cellphone. She had her front door key and, thank heavens, a small cash float. She and Jemima called it their running away money. They never, ever went out anywhere without enough money to take a taxi

home. Though this was the first time that Izzy had
ever had to use it.

Shoes in hand, she tiptoed out of the room. She
seemed to be at the bottom of some stairs, with
a light on a half-landing above. Cautiously she
went up, ears strained. But the house was silent
except for the ticking of a big grandfather clock
somewhere. Before she saw that, however, she
saw a big front door, with leaded lights and some
impressive locks.

Izzy skidded across a slippery black and white
floor, fumbled the locks and dived out into the
street. It did not occur to her, until the front door
had closed behind her, that it was the silliest thing
she could possibly have done.

She did not know where she was. She was
dressed in only the flimsiest clothes. It was the
sort of thing that all the personal safety notices
warned you about. But anything, absolutely anything, felt better than having to face the man
whose jacket she had purloined. Whose mouth
she had kissed with abandon. Whom she had just
happened to cast as her Fantasy of the Day.

Izzy could have groaned aloud.

She didn't. Instead, she set her teeth and
marched firmly down the street, looking fierce.
The ferocity was not entirely to repel attackers,
either. Izzy was furious with herself.

So furious, indeed, that she was hardly grateful for her luck when she found herself in Knightsbridge, where there were several international hotels and black taxis cruised all through the night.

She was home by half past four.

She looked wincingly at the fridge. She longed for a cheese sandwich. She knew she ought to have something to eat. Tonight's fiasco had to have something to do with the lack of food. But cheese made you dream, didn't it?

'Enough dreams already,' said Izzy grimly.

She compromised with a couple of pints of water and a mug of hot milk, and took herself off to bed, muttering.

She was gone! Dom could not believe it. He had put her in the study, like a gentleman, not so much as slid that scrap of scarlet provocation off her delicious body. And now, in the morning, he found she had thrown his jacket on the floor and left without a forwarding address.

'That's the last time I behave like a gentleman,' he told the mirror ferociously.

With Molly di Peretti, however, he was more circumspect. So circumspect, indeed, that she entirely misunderstood his motive for calling.

'So you want to do the party circuit after all, do you?' she said tolerantly. 'Enjoy yourself last night?'

Dom ground his teeth but kept his own counsel. 'Very much.' He was not going to tell anyone that his lady in red had decamped without his getting so much as a name or a phone number out of her.

His scruples had not been so nice that he hadn't looked in that silly little bag before he left her sleeping. But it had revealed nothing. Not so much as a credit card with her name on. Just a key, lipgloss, a couple of bank notes and a tiny phial of perfume. He could still smell the perfume. If he did not find her, he thought, that perfume would haunt him for the rest of his life.

Only, of course, he *was* going to find her.

So he said to Molly di Peretti, 'I'm sorry I've been such a pain. Jay was quite right. I'll do whatever you say.'

'He said *what*?' said Jay Christopher and Abby in unison, when Molly reported this unlikely conversation.

She repeated it.

'He's up to something,' said his fond sister positively.

'That's what I thought,' agreed Molly. 'But he came round this morning, meek as a lamb, and went through the press cuttings with me. Learned all the names on the guest list. The full works.'

Abby's eyes narrowed. '*Definitely* up to something. He told me he was much too busy to make time for a PR campaign.'

Jay was more optimistic. 'So now he's had time to think about it, he's seen that it's worth making the time. Now it's up to us to prove that's right.'

'You,' pointed out Abby bitterly, 'don't have to design the campaign—or make Dom co-operate.'

'He's falling over himself to co-operate,' said Jay airily.

Abby shook her head. 'No matter what he says now, he won't stay obliging. Dom and compromise are strangers to each other.'

Molly had been thinking. Now she tipped her chair back and stared at the ceiling with narrowed eyes. 'Okay. Dom doesn't do compromise. How is he on delivering his side of the bargain?'

Abby sighed. 'Oh, he keeps his promises.' She looked at her friend curiously. 'You're not seriously thinking of trawling for a blonde film star for him, are you Moll?'

Molly let her chair come back to earth with a thud. 'Not a blonde film star,' she said with relish.

'But I can do you a very nice line in red-headed models.'

Jay snapped his fingers. 'Jemima Dare! Of course. Molly, you're inspired!'

Abby looked worried. 'Dom doesn't do blind dates, either.'

Molly grinned from ear to ear. 'This is not a blind date. What I have in mind is a whole lot more exciting than that.'

Abby groaned. 'Well, Dom does exciting, all right,' she admitted.

Jay was beaming. 'I like it. Two problems. One solution. Neat. Very neat.'

'That's what I thought,' agreed Molly. 'She might even turn up this time, if I tell her manager that I've got Jemima a big strong man to jump with.'

Abby was alarmed. 'Jump? Jump where?'

The others ignored her. Jay said, 'Blane's in Australia. You'll have to speak to the PA. Or Jemima herself.'

Molly pulled a face. 'Couple of flakes. She's got a sister who's pretty together, though. I might call her.'

'Jump *where*?' yelled Abby.

Jay looked at her in mild surprise. 'Chelsea Bridge.'

'She's jumping off Chelsea Bridge?' gasped Abby, horrified.

'No, no. It's one of those bungee jump things. Full safety harness.'

'And a pile of society photographers for her to land on if it breaks,' said Molly with a grin. 'And now Dom will be her consolation,' she added, bubbling over at the thought.

Abby closed her eyes. 'If you think that, you're crazy.'

'Well, he looks good. All tough and outdoorsy. Not at all the pretty boy-band type she usually hangs with,' said Molly, whose taste ran to leather-clad drummers—or had until she'd met and fallen in love with a car-mad computer genius. 'Be an experience for her.'

Abby opened her eyes. 'Oh, it will be that, all right,' she said. 'Jumping off a crane with my brother Dominic in a right royal temper. That's an experience I wouldn't wish on my worst enemy.'

'It will be good for her,' said Molly callously. 'The moment Jemima Dare got that big contract she turned into a total pain in the ass.'

Jay nodded sadly.

Molly bared her teeth. 'Frankly, Abby, if your brother Dominic cuts her down to size, I'll personally contribute to his expedition. Put me down for a pair of the best snow shoes money can buy.'

But tender-hearted Abby shook her head. 'You don't know Dom. All I can say is: Jemima Dare has my sympathy!'

The next week passed in a rush for Izzy.

Just as well, really, she thought. Every time she stopped, her late night adventure returned to make her jump and sweat. It was like having a splinter—most of the time you could ignore it, but when you stopped to think you knew it was still there. Still hurting. And probably going deeper.

'It is not going deeper,' said Izzy aloud with great firmness.

Okay, she still dreamed about those heated kisses. Her own abandon. That, of course, was the masked ball of the unconscious, and probably pure fantasy.

But the thing that really brought her up short, and made her exclaim aloud if she wasn't careful, was a laughing dark chocolate voice saying in horror, 'A *sonnet*?' That wasn't fantasy. That was horribly like real life.

The more she thought about it, the more convinced she was that she had flung herself at a living, breathing man. Who had taken her home and tucked her up safe. On whom she had run out without so much as a note of explanation. Whose face she could not even remember. And who still haunted her dreams.

'Ouch,' shouted Izzy, bouncing out of her chair so hard that she knocked it over.

Pepper looked up from her desk.

'Problem?'

Izzy subsided. 'Nothing I can't handle.' She hoped that was true.

'You sure? You look as if you're drowning over there.'

Izzy returned to the subject of work with relief. 'When the woman from the PR company told me that the launch was just the start, I didn't know what she meant,' she told Pepper with feeling. 'Now I do. The phone just doesn't stop. It's great.'

But Pepper, infinitely more experienced in business than her cousin, was more temperate.

'That's good. But we mustn't let it take our eye off the ball. Publicity will be no use at all if the catalogue isn't out and the goods aren't ready. Hire an assistant if you need one. But for God's sake don't fall behind on the production schedule.'

Izzy chuckled. 'Okay, boss.'

So when Molly rang up, asking whether Jemima was available, Izzy cut her short.

'Jemima only did the launch as a one-off,' she said pleasantly, but with finality.

'But she is back in the country?' pressed Molly.

Izzy looked at her wall calendar. 'Due in six a.m. flight from Rio de Janeiro tomorrow. I'll see her at breakfast.'

'Well, could you ask her to give me a call? Soonest! Tell her,' said Molly tantalisingly, 'that it's good news.'

Izzy wrote it down on her daily organiser and transferred it to the kitchen noticeboard that night. But when she got up in the morning there was no suitcase in the hall. Jemima's door still stood open and the bedroom was untenanted.

'Flight delay?' said Pepper.

Izzy agreed. But she was uneasy, though she could not have said why.

When the day had passed and there was no message from Jemima, she looked up the flight details on the Internet. The plane had landed on time!

Thoroughly unsettled, she called Jemima's cellphone. It was switched off. So then she called her sister's agency. It was a frustrating experience. In the end she slammed the phone down.

'What is going *on*?' she exclaimed, torn between exasperation and real unease.

Pepper was frowning over a new designer's portfolio. She put it down, eyebrows raised.

'Trouble?'

'Jemima isn't still in Brazil,' said Izzy, breathing hard. 'According to Dolly Daydream on Reception at the model agency, she's back in the UK. Everyone else is too cagey to say where she is.'

'So?'

'It's not like her.' Izzy bit her lip, trying to marshal her thoughts. 'Even if she had to go straight to another job she'd call. She always calls.'

Pepper shrugged.

'And before she went away she was sounding—odd. On edge.'

Pepper looked at her curiously. 'You're very protective.'

'Older sister syndrome,' said Izzy brusquely.

Pepper was an only child. 'It's not a criticism, Izzy. I think it's nice. But Jemima is her own woman. She doesn't have to check in with us before she goes off somewhere.' She gave Izzy an encouraging grin. 'Hey, maybe she met a great guy and just wanted to party with him.'

'Maybe…'

Izzy shut her eyes. *Oh, Jemima Jane, where are you? Something has gone wrong with you. I can feel it.*

Pepper whipped a press cutting off the wall behind her and waved it under Izzy's nose. Izzy did not have to read it. They had laughed about it when it had first come out, all three of them. A dazzled journalist had written:

> *Jemima Dare is more than a hot babe. There's the gut-wrenching sensuality. And, then again, there's the unreachability, Titania's ethereal provocation. There's the tremulous, tender mouth—allied to a siren's body. The sexual punch is deadly. And then you think—will she be gentle with her victims?*

Oh, yes, they had all laughed—Jemima longest of all. And now Pepper was saying tolerantly, 'Jemima just hit the big time. She isn't going to want to take in pizza and a movie with the family the first time she gets back to London.'

Izzy opened her eyes. 'You don't understand.'

'What's not to understand? She doesn't mean to be mean. Give it time; the gloss will wear off.'

'But you don't know her like I do,' said Izzy, still worried. 'This just isn't Jemima.'

'Hey,' said Pepper gently. 'Success changes people.'

'Not that much,' Izzy said stubbornly.

Pepper patted her shoulder. 'You're a good sister, Izzy. Do you give the same service to cousins? I could do with someone like you in my corner, believing in me right or wrong.'

Izzy struggled with herself. 'You've got it.' But her smile was perfunctory.

Pepper pursed her lips. 'You're serious about this,' she said on a note of discovery.

Izzy pushed her hand through her hair. 'I knew there was something wrong,' she said with difficulty. 'When Jay Jay was here for the launch, I knew. There wasn't time to talk. But I knew. We were so busy. Oh, I should have *made* time.'

'Okay. You've got a feeling. I'll buy that.' Pepper was suddenly brisk. 'So we find out where she is and you go talk to her.'

Izzy gave her a slightly watery smile. 'Thanks. Only how? The agency won't even talk to me.'

'I'll call in a couple of favours. I've been in this business a long time. And I'm the name behind the revolution in retail shopping,' said Pepper with superb assurance. 'There's someone out there who will tell me where the face of Belinda is hiding out.'

And why? said Izzy. But she did not say it aloud.

Pepper did not overestimate her abilities. Within three hours she was pushing an address across the desk. It was a boutique hotel in an exclusive area of London.

'Seems you're right.' There was an apologetic note in her voice.

Izzy stared at the address. 'She's staying at a hotel? But why? I don't understand.'

Pepper said uncomfortably, 'Well, she's not alone.'

'So?' Izzy was impatient. 'What am I? Victorian? I don't care who she's with. I just want to know she's all right.'

Pepper drew a deep breath. 'According to my information, she arrived hiding behind dark glasses and hasn't been out of the suite since.' Her voice was completely neutral. 'She booked in under an assumed name, too.'

'*What?*'

'I guess she's been on what Steven would call the bender of a lifetime,' Pepper said gently. 'She's probably ashamed of herself. That's why she hasn't called.'

She made Izzy a cup of coffee in silent sympathy. And then, because she had done all she could, went back to work.

Stunned, Izzy drank the coffee and tried to get her head round this new, irresponsible Jemima.

And when she couldn't, she went back to work, too.

Izzy was nothing if not practical. If Jemima wanted help she would call. If she didn't, then she was sorting out her own problems—whatever they were. She wasn't a child. And Izzy wasn't her keeper.

It still cost her a sleepless night.

And in the sleepless hours, to her dismay, the image of her alien lover came back to haunt her with might-have-been. Well, not the image, exactly. She still could not remember a thing about what he looked like. But there was a memory of strength, of wicked laughter, and the fatally alluring sensation that they belonged together.

'I wish,' said Izzy wryly.

In the dark she sat up in bed and hugged her knees. Pepper had her Steven to hold hands with when life went wrong. Jemima presumably had the man who hired luxurious hotel suites for her. Izzy had to stand on her own two flat feet and fight right back. And, just for a moment, she wanted a hand to hold and a shoulder to lean against more than anything in the world.

She would not have admitted it to anyone else. Hell, she would not even have admitted it to herself if it weren't five o'clock in the morning and she weren't in turmoil. But that momentary sense of belonging, of being part of a team, of knowing there was someone she could utterly, totally trust, had been bliss. Ever since she had tiptoed out of that unknown house she had been in mourning for the dream she'd left behind.

'Tosh,' Izzy had told herself robustly on an hourly basis ever since.

But now, alone in the small hours, and worried out of her mind about Jemima, there was nothing she wanted more than to have the dream back.

She took herself to task. That's exactly why romance rots the brain. You don't need a white knight on a charger to gallop up and take over. You need to get yourself sorted, she told herself hardily. And if that means making a fool of yourself and turning up uninvited at Jemima's love-nest, so be it.

So that was the decision taken, it seemed. Izzy gave a great sigh, as if a burden had slid off her back. And fell asleep at last.

Of course it was not as easy as that. She had no trouble convincing Pepper that she needed to be out of the office for a couple of hours. But getting into Jemima's suite was another thing altogether.

The hotel denied all knowledge of Jemima Dare. Izzy walked up and down outside three times in the morning sunshine, calling herself all sorts of a fool. Nobody else thought there was anything wrong. So why was she punishing herself like this?

She was hot. She was sweaty. She was wearing the wrong shoes. She could feel a fine new blister beginning to throb. The doorman at a nearby gaming club was starting to look at her suspiciously. And *still* she could not make up her mind to stop fussing and go home.

'I need my head examined,' she muttered.

She tried Jemima's cellphone number again. Phone still switched off. Of course she might just be lost in the romantic idyll of the century. Only the hairs on the back of Izzy's neck said that Jemima was isolated and in deep, deep trouble.

She could be wrong. She and Jemima were no longer as close as they had been as infants, as teenagers. It was all too possible that she was wrong. *Please let me be wrong.*

Izzy stopped trying to connect to Jemima's number. The little telephone slipped in her wet hand. It was so hot she could barely think straight.

'I need water,' said Izzy aloud.

She bought a bottle from a street vendor and went into the park. Children were playing on the dry grass. Lovers wandered hand in hand, or sat and gazed silently into each other's eyes. Dogs romped. Even men in business suits on their way to somewhere else seemed to slow down and look around at the trees with pleasure. Izzy felt like the only person in the world who wasn't happy on this perfect day.

Was she being a fool after all? Had Jemima turned into just another celebrity, with no time for anyone who was not a celebrity, too? The idea hurt, but she had to be realistic. It was obviously what Pepper thought. Even her parents weren't worried.

Izzy looked round the park and the voices in her head receded. Maybe everyone else was right. But she had loved Jemima from the moment she was born. She did not believe it.

She stood up. *If I'm a fool, I'm a fool. But I'm going in there.*

It was not easy. The hotel prided itself on its luxurious intimacy. Which meant that it was small and the desk staff knew everyone staying there. Especially as half of them were the sort of stars that made Jemima Dare's new celebrity look pretty pale. But in an adventurous life Izzy had got herself into—and out of—stickier situations than infiltrating a luxury hotel at the tail end of the tourist season.

List your advantages, then use them. Izzy repeated the mantra that had got her out of the tightest spots in her life.

She pulled a face. Even now, some of those spots could give her nightmares if she let them. But she was here, and alive, and she knew she could get in to see Jemima if she put her mind to it.

Her advantages were—well, she was tall and athletic. She had the sort of devil-may-care smile that made people smile back at her in the street. Okay, she wasn't in Jemima's class, but she had the same silky red hair and long legs. Maybe she didn't pack Jemima's sexual punch, but people *liked* her. She had charmed her way out of more tight corners than Jemima had any idea of.

And then it hit her. *The same silky red hair!*

Izzy went as taut as a bowstring.

Right!

Rapidly she took stock. She knew she could imitate Jemima's model-girl slinky walk. She'd done it at last year's Christmas party and Jemima had laughed until her mascara ran. As for the make-up—well, Jemima might threaten her with make-up lessons, but Izzy had lived with Jemima long enough to learn the rudiments.

I just bet I can do that tremulous, tender mouth thing if I put my mind to it, she thought. All it takes is a lot of lippy—and a serious attitude adjustment, of course.

The reflection cheered her up. She certainly ought to be able to fool a hotel desk clerk into thinking she was Jemima returning to her room. Or she ought to if she kept moving and didn't let her innate honesty trap her into giving herself away.

'I can do this,' said Izzy aloud.

Fifteen minutes later she was standing outside the hotel. After a visit to a make-up counter and the ladies' room of a coffee shop, her hair seemed to have trebled in size, along with her eyelashes and her pouting lips.

She made one last attempt to call her sister. Same result. Izzy knew she had no choice. She either did it or gave up on Jemima. And Izzy was not a natural giver-upper.

'Okay,' she said, putting back her shoulders and going into catwalk motion. 'You're on.'

She wriggled the short sleeves of her cotton top off her shoulders. It was not much, but it was all she could think of to give her that little-girl-lost sexiness that was Jemima's trademark. She fluffed up her hair. *Think ethereal provocation, Isabel! You're gentle with your victims, remember.*

She snorted in derision. Pulled a face. Squared her shoulders. And launched herself into Operation Rescue Jay Jay.

It was easier than she had dared hope. The reception desk was dealing with a couple of guests who were clearly demanding all their concentration. A speeding porter said, 'Good afternoon, Ms Blane,' which meant that Jemima was staying here under the name of her manager—Basil Blane. Izzy was taken aback. She disliked Blane and had thought Jemima felt the same.

Still, no time to think about that now. Nobody else took any notice of her at all. Izzy was outside the suite in seconds. She knocked.

Nothing happened. She could not hear any sounds from inside the room. Izzy's heart began to pound uncomfortably. She knocked again, their special knock this time, the one without which nobody had ever been admitted to their attic playroom. Still no answer. She was thinking—service entrance? Fire escape?—when there was a sudden crashing noise, as if someone had knocked over a load of furniture, and the door was flung open.

'Izzy? *Izzy?*'

It was Jemima—not ethereal any longer, not even beautiful, but a starveling thing, with hollow cheeks and wild eyes. Her hands wouldn't keep still and she was panting.

'My God,' said Izzy involuntarily, 'what have you done to yourself?'

In only a week or so it seemed as if Jemima had lost half her body weight.

Izzy just stood there and stared, going colder and colder inside. Her instincts had been right—in spades. This was *bad*.

'Jay Jay—'

Jemima gave a banshee wail and flung herself into Izzy's stunned arms.

'Oh, thank God. Thank God. Oh, Izzy, you've got to help me! I'm going out of my mind!'

It took Izzy about ten minutes to establish that Jemima was not exaggerating. And that things were a lot, lot worse than the worst she had imagined.

'We're getting out of here—now,' she said firmly.

But Jemima—beautiful, confident, successful Jemima—huddled into the corner and wouldn't get up from the floor. She sat on the deep pile luxury carpet as if it was a stone prison floor and whimpered that she couldn't—she couldn't. Basil would find her!

'So?' said Izzy, her fingers flexing. She quite looked forward to Basil finding them. *Nobody* did this to her sister and got away with it.

Jemima was white to the hairline. She put up a hand to ease her throat. 'I'm under contract. He *owns* me. The Belinda people will have me

thrown in prison. I'll never work again.'
Jemima's voice rose to hysteria pitch.

There was obviously no point in trying to reason with her.

So Izzy did what she always did when Jemima was in a state. Took the heat out of the situation, talked calmly, made her laugh a little. Eventually she coaxed her out of the corner. Then she sat on the couch with her and took hold of Jemima's hand comfortingly.

'Do you remember your first day in kindergarten?' she said, teasing.

Jemima managed a watery smile. 'You said there was nothing to be afraid of. People were nice really.' Her smile died. 'But they're not, Izzy. Basil's right. It's a jungle out there. I need him to look after me.' She started to shiver, in spite of the late summer sunshine.

Izzy wanted to *kill*. 'Basil's a shark,' she said coldly. 'You don't need anyone to look after you but yourself.'

But Jemima just shivered harder.

In the end, Izzy switched tack and brought in reinforcements. Pepper's Steven was the Master of an Oxford College.

'You must know some seriously discreet doctors,' she told him in a rapid phone call. 'My sister is gibbering and she says it's the end of her career if she moves from this hotel room. I don't know what to do.'

Steven knew a lot of troubled students, as well as members of the medical profession.

'What's she taken?' he said practically.

'*Taken?*' Izzy was shocked. 'Jemima doesn't do drugs. Never has.'

But the moment he said it, it made sense. She looked at her sister, with a cushion clutched protectively to her chest and her eyes darting all over the place, and suddenly everything fell into place.

'I'll call you back.'

She cut the call and sank down on the carpet in front of Jemima.

'Tell me the truth, Jay Jay,' she said gently. 'Has he been making you take something?'

Jemima swallowed. 'I was putting on weight. Basil says every pound shows on the camera.'

So that explained how her gorgeous sister had turned skeletal. Izzy added another score to Basil Blane's tally.

She said in a neutral voice, 'So what did he give you? Pills? An injection?'

'Pills,' admitted Jemima. She blew her nose. 'They make me feel *awful*,' she burst out.

'I can see that.' Izzy thought fast. 'We need to get you to a doctor *now*.'

But at once Jemima took fright again, shrinking back among the cushions as if Izzy were her enemy. It took what seemed like hours to coax her out of her panic. And even longer to get her to the door, even after Steven had rung back with the name of a doctor who would see her at once, if Izzy could get her to his consulting room.

'Basil will find out. He'll come after me,' said Jemima. 'He said I wasn't to leave the room unless his PA was with me. He calls me all the time to check. And to tell me what to do next.'

She could not keep her eyes or her hands still. For a moment Izzy nearly despaired. It was not a feeling she was used to. She was not a woman who gave up on things.

But there seemed no way to reach Jemima in this state. Logic didn't work. Common sense didn't work. Even a sharp slap, to shock her out of incipient hysterics, only resulted in Jemima collapsing in a soggy heap on the carpet again.

'Damn,' said Izzy, nursing her smarting palm and not liking herself very much.

In the end she did the only thing she could, and stepped through into her sister's irrational, obsessed world.

'Okay, I got in here pretending to be you. I'll stay and carry on pretending. Until you're safe anyway.'

For the first time a tiny flicker of hope ignited in Jemima's eyes. 'Can you?' she said doubtfully.

Izzy's chin came up. 'With a bit of luck and a following wind.'

'But I'm never lucky,' said Jemima, starting to shake again.

Izzy put her hands on her shoulders and looked deep into her sister's eyes. 'You make your own luck,' she said steadily. 'Between us, you and I can do anything.'

Jemima gave a long, long sigh. 'Oh, Izzy. You're so strong.'

A treacherous thought nudged its way into the corner of Izzy's mind: *You wouldn't say that if you'd seen me melting to a voice like warm chocolate. And not knowing whether it was truth or a dream.*

She cleared her throat. 'Um—sometimes.'

And she squashed the sneaking, shameful thought that she would melt all over again if she ever got the chance.

CHAPTER FOUR

'Dom, you're impossible!'

Dominic skidded out from under the beaten-up Jeep, found a spanner, and disappeared again.

A muffled voice drifted back to Abby. 'Sorry about that.'

'No, you're not,' she said. 'You didn't even think about it.' Hands on hips, she glared down at the long legs sticking out from under the elderly vehicle. 'And another thing—those jeans are disgusting.'

Her brother ignored that. Typical, thought Abby.

She tried again. 'It's only half a day. You can afford half a day, surely?'

'Why should I?'

She hunkered down and peered under the Jeep. 'Because it's good publicity. Because Molly's gone to a lot of trouble to set this up.'

Dominic's reply was muffled. Abby was sure he couldn't actually have said what she thought he said: 'She hasn't set me up with the one person I want her to.'

She said, 'Because you *promised*.'

99

Dominic said something very rude which Abby could not make out. She did not ask him to repeat it.

'The expedition still needs funding,' she said, concentrating on the main issue. 'You've said it yourself. There are too many people out there trying to get sponsorship. You've got to get *noticed*.'

Dom put up his arms and wheeled himself out again. He sat up and looped long arms about his crossed knees.

'You're trying to turn me into a performing flea again.'

She ignored the warning note. 'You said you'd do it if C&C came up with a woman.'

He pulled a face. 'Don't like the sound of that.'

'Maybe not,' said Abby with resolution. 'But that's what you said. Are you backing out now?'

Their eyes met with a clash that recalled every battle over the old rocking horse they had ever had. It was too much for Dominic's sense of humour.

'Hate bossy women,' he said, grinning.

Abby suppressed a sigh of relief and grinned back. 'You hate any woman with a mind of her own.'

He looked wounded. 'That's not true.'

Abby refrained from listing his most recent girlfriends. Instead she applied herself to Molly di Peretti's comprehensive briefing. 'Jemima Dare isn't bossy, anyway. She's—'

Abby thought of all the things that Molly had said—ego-driven, temperamental, a flake. No, maybe those were not the things to tell Dom. She fell back on an edited version of the truth.

'She's going to have to do this bungee jump thing and she's terrified.' Well, that was a reasonable assumption. And Dom was chivalrous. Sometimes. An appeal to his protective side might just work. 'She needs her hand held.'

Dominic saw through her, as he always did. His grey eyes danced. '"Dominic Templeton-Burke, babysitter",' he mused. 'Yup. I can see that getting the headlines.'

Abby curbed her exasperation. 'Stop trying to wind me up. The girl is gorgeous. And totally hot just now. Get your arms round her. Look macho. You'll get more than headlines. You'll get *photographs*.'

'Macho?' said Dominic, affronted.

'Oh, come on Dom. You know the sort of thing. Professional gear. Plenty of muscles. Don't shave for a couple of days. Oh, and try and look noble.'

He pulled a face. But he also laughed aloud and stopped teasing. 'Okay. I get the picture. You want me to give this bird the full mountain rescue treatment.'

His sister looked at him suspiciously. 'I want you to look strong and male and amazingly competent,' she said.

Experience had taught her that with Dom it was wise to spell out the terms of the contract. He was quite capable of turning the wretched Jemima into a backpack substitute and abseiling down the side of the nearest building with her flung over his shoulder.

'No tricks. No jokes. I want you to look like the sort of man who could get a woman out of anything, if he put his mind to it. Real fantasy hero stuff.'

Dominic pursed his lips. 'Ah. A St George for the twenty-first century. I see.'

Abby was alarmed. She knew her brother. 'No swords. No armour,' she said warningly.

He made a face. 'You're no fun. I thought this was all about *pretending*.'

Abby winced. It was not easy to ask Dominic about his feelings. He had a way of suddenly going inside himself, leaving just a charming mask doing the talking. It chilled even his sister, who was probably closer to him than anyone else. But, close as they were, there were areas of his life through which Abby walked on tiptoe. Under the sharp wit, Dom was a loyal and protective brother—but he could be savage in protecting himself from intruders. Most people backed away, sooner or later, including the girlfriends. Well, maybe particularly the girlfriends. But Abby loved him.

She said gently, 'You'd both be pretending, Dom. It isn't as if she's setting a trap to catch you.'

'You mean like trying to get my older brother jealous?' His voice was light but his eyes were hard.

'Oh, Dom! Kelly was a one-off.'

'Yes?' He had that look, the one she dreaded, the look of a fortress: drawbridge up, portcullis coming down; try and slide underneath it and I'll cut you to ribbons.

But still she tried. 'Most women are as honest as you are.'

His face was stone.

'Look—I'm not like Kelly, am I? I couldn't pretend to love a man because I wanted to use him as a stepping stone to get to another guy. None of my friends would either.'

He relaxed. 'No. But you're a sweetheart.'

'And my friends—'

He flung up a hand. 'And you see the best in people. I'll buy you as the last honest woman in London. The jury's out on your friends.'

'But—'

'Quit while you're ahead, kid. I'm not changing. I know myself. And I'm not letting you fix me up with some foxy lady. Not even for a long weekend.'

Abby bit her lip. 'I didn't mean—'

'Yes, you did,' said Dominic calmly. 'And it's okay. It was a long time ago and I'm over it. More than that. I learned a valuable lesson.'

Abby was cautious. 'Which is?'

'Never trust a woman with anything important,' he said. 'They have their own agenda. And loyalty ain't on it.'

It broke her heart. 'Oh, *Dom*!'

He gave her a sudden grin. 'Don't look like that. I can live with it. There's lots of gorgeous women out there just waiting for me not to trust them.'

Abby began to be alarmed. 'Not Jemima Dare.'

'Why not?'

His mouth was beginning to curl wickedly. It was a look that Abby knew well. Her heart sank.

She threw in her last shot. 'No point in trying to sweep her off her feet, anyway. She'll be wise to you. You've already met her.'

He frowned. 'I have?'

'It's in the press cuttings file, apparently. She was at the Best of British Awards. You sat on the same table. You even danced with her a couple of times.'

He thought about it. 'What's the name again?'

Abby glared. 'Jemima Dare. The face of Belinda. You must know her. She's on every hoarding between Hyde Park Corner and Heathrow.'

He shook his head, frowning. 'Don't remember—' Then he snapped his fingers. 'Got it. Dance in February. Skinny redhead. Too much make-up, not enough dress. Kept falling off her shoes.'

'And—?' prompted Abby.

'And—?' he echoed, mock innocent.

'What happened? Did you like her?'

He shrugged. 'She was quite a nice kid, I suppose.'

Abby did not know whether she was disappointed or relieved. 'No chemistry, then?'

Dominic laughed heartily at the thought.

'But you will go and do the bungee jump tomorrow?' she pressed.

The secret laughter was back. 'Oh, yes, I'll go. I shall enjoy it.'

Quite suddenly Abby found she believed him. It was not an encouraging thought.

Pepper was incensed.

'Pretend to be Jemima? Oh, come on, Izzy. How long do you think you will get away with that?'

'Long enough.'

'And you think people won't notice? Photographers know when their models gain a pound.'

'I'm not doing a photographic shoot,' explained Izzy. 'Just sitting here taking Beastly Basil's phone calls. You know nobody can tell our voices apart on the phone.'

'You mean her diary is empty?' Pepper was scornful.

'She's doing a bungee jump for charity tomorrow. I can manage that. Nobody looks their best flying out on the end of a gigantic elastic band. And after that she'll be safe in her clinic and it doesn't matter if Beastly Basil finds out she's gone.'

'You're crazy.' Pepper sighed. 'Well, okay, I guess I can't order you to come back to work.' It sounded as if she would have liked to. 'But it's back to normal on Monday, right? *Out of the Attic* needs you.'

'Okay, boss.'

She spent a lot of that day looking at Jemima's portfolio and practising the various make-up tricks she had seen Jemima use. There were not many clothes in her sister's wardrobe that fitted her. But in the end Izzy managed to put together an outfit that would look okay for a model girl on her first bungee jump.

Though she had second thoughts when she looked at them next morning. The leather trousers were just a little too tight. Last night they had felt like body armour, even though she'd teamed them with a floaty transparent top. The long sleeves looked as if they were already in rags. They also left her shoulders bare. The thing had a plunging neckline that her mother would undoubtedly say was indecent. But at least it was not—quite—too tight. And as long as everyone focused on her cleavage, they wouldn't be looking at her face and seeing that it was not the perfect oval that Jemima Dare was known for.

'Sorted,' said Izzy—and went to wash her hair with Jemima's exclusive salon preparations.

She had watched her sister do her hair a thousand times. Izzy stuck her tongue between her teeth and concentrated on the nice placing of heated rollers until her arms started to shake.

'Blasted models. Blasted hair,' she muttered.

But it worked. When she stood looking at herself in the mirror, it was as near as dammit Jay Jay who looked back—feathery auburn hair, sequinned trainers and all. Izzy looked down at these last. They had seemed to select themselves.

'Madness,' she said wryly. But at least she was wearing her own underwear.

Then she looked at herself critically. Not bad. Not bad at all. She struck an attitude.

'Jemima Dare Mark II is holding up just fine. And ready for business,' she announced.

She did a soft shoe shuffle. The basic design of the shoes might have been intended for the running track, but these had twinkling lights at the heel and a dusting of hearts and stars on the uppers. Even the laces glittered. Oh, well, as long as people looked at the extravagant gear they wouldn't notice any discrepancies between the model they were expecting and the one they actually got, Izzy comforted herself.

But she would be glad when it was over. Quite apart from all the lying, she just didn't understand how Jemima could stand this boring life. Hours and hours and *hours* in front of the mirror, and absolutely no sense of achievement at the end of it!

Oh, well, at least the bungee jump wouldn't be boring, exactly. Though she had trouble drumming up the nerves her minder clearly expected.

'Butterflies?' he said, ushering her protectively into the car.

Would Jemima be scared? Probably. She had no great head for heights. Whereas Izzy had tried parachute jumping without a qualm.

She shrugged. 'I can handle it,' she said evasively, trying to copy Jemima's manner.

Josh, the PR company's minder, didn't seem to notice anything wrong. He didn't try to make conversation on the way to the jump site either. In fact, in the car he sent her one or two glances that were distinctly nervous. Didn't he and Jemima get on?

Izzy would have tried to find out, just to make sure she kept in character. Only she didn't want to take any unnecessary risks. So she gave Josh the up and under smile that Jemima had perfected.

'This is a first for me,' she said truthfully.

Josh relaxed. 'At least you won't be on your own.'

'No,' agreed Izzy dryly. 'Here come the usual suspects,' she added, using Jemima's phrase for the press pack.

The limo was pulling into the jump site. There was a clutch of eager groupies, a greeter or two looking welcoming, and about a dozen photographers, expressionless as always.

Only this time there was someone else. Not a groupie, not a greeter, and definitely not a photographer. He stood behind the crowd, watching them ironically.

Stood? No, he lounged in the shadows, his arms crossed over a powerful chest and a derisive tilt to his sculpted mouth. There was something about that mouth that shocked Izzy into total awareness.

'*What is that?*' she said in a voice like cracked glass. Suddenly she was all Izzy. Not a hint of Jemima's clipped sophistication left.

Josh jumped. 'What?'

'The sneer on legs.'

He looked round wildly. '*What?*'

'The man leaning against the wall,' said Izzy tautly. 'Over there.'

Josh followed her gesture. 'Oh, Dominic Templeton-Burke,' he said, clearly relieved to be asked a question he could answer. He grinned. 'Your date for the day.'

Izzy felt her mouth dry. *I don't believe it. I'm going to be unmasked in front of a hundred cameras?*

'Date?' she said ominously.

Josh went back to jumpy mode. 'After the—er—misunderstandings last time, Culp and Christopher thought you'd like an escort,' he gabbled.

Izzy looked at him narrowly. You could almost see the piece of paper he was reading from, she thought.

'Very kind of them,' she said dryly. 'Now tell me the truth.'

'That is the truth.'

'I don't believe you.'

But there was no time to get the truth out of Josh. The car was drawing to a halt while the man watched it, his expression just short of mockery. Izzy felt as if he could see right through the windows and past Josh's head, straight into her brain.

He'll know I'm not Jemima, she thought in a panic. *He'll tell.*

She said, 'Nobody mentioned a date. Why the hell—? Who is he again?'

Josh looked at her curiously. 'Dominic Templeton-Burke,' he said again, enunciating clearly, as if she had a hangover. Or as if she were being seriously difficult.

Seriously difficult was good, thought Izzy. You could probably get away with a lot if people thought you had a point to prove about your own celebrity status. She decided to be a spoilt celebrity in spades.

She pouted. 'This is a name I should know?'

He went deadpan and patient. 'The explorer?' The car stopped and he leaned forward to open the door. 'I thought you two were great friends.'

It was just as well he was not looking at her, thought Izzy. She was sure that Jemima would never let her jaw drop like that.

Oh great, she thought. A blind date she wasn't expecting—and with a man who knew Jemima! Only, just how well did he know Jemima, come to think of it?

Izzy didn't know his name. But all that meant was that Jemima had not spoken of him, or not that Izzy could recall. That in turn meant one of two things: either Jemima hardly knew him at all, or she knew him so well—or wanted to, anyway—that he was not a subject for family discussion.

Oh boy! I should have known things were falling into place too easily. Nothing ever goes that well.

Josh opened the door and got out. Izzy leaned forward to take a good look at her Nemesis.

He might have walked straight out of a bad dream. Oh, not that he wasn't handsome in a spare, rangy sort of way. Or what she could see of him was handsome. He had dark untidy hair, high cheekbones, and a haughty, uncompromising mouth. Oh, yes, she could see Jemima going for a man like that, all right. Sexy as hell, lord of all he surveyed. Izzy's heart sank. Yes, that was just Jemima's style.

Whereas he was not the sort of man that Izzy was attracted to at all. As she looked at him all the hairs on the back of her neck stood up in alarm. Handsome, yes. And tough as they come. From his camouflage gear to his wrap-around shades he was the stuff of nightmares.

Well, Izzy's nightmares. To be precise, her most secret nightmares. The ones she didn't tell about. Not anyone. Not ever.

In the act of getting out of Culp and Christopher's stretched limousine, Izzy froze. Something very like panic trickled down her spine.

Josh stuck his head back in the car. 'You okay?'

No. I'm terrified all of a sudden. And not of the damned jump.

'I'm fine. Just—' She looked at the structure from which she was supposed to jump and was inspired. 'It's just that it's so *high*.'

Josh gave her what he must have thought was a reassuring smile. 'Just as well that you've got Dominic to hold your hand, then.'

Izzy frowned. 'Hold my hand?'

'He's going to jump, too. With you,' ended Josh in congratulatory tones. 'That's the point. You've got an escort all the way down to the bottom.'

'Oh,' said Izzy faintly.

If he noticed that she looked sick, Josh must have put it down to fear of heights. Whereas Izzy's fear was a lot nearer home—and advancing imminently.

With a visible shrug, Dominic Templeton-Burke stopped leaning against the wall and moved towards them. Izzy watched the careless, confident stride and her heart dropped like a stone. It was worse than a swagger. Swaggerers she could deal with. But that effortless superiority was something else. She wasn't even going to try to deal with that.

'He's going to jump, too? You mean with me? *Together?*'

Josh nodded, pleased.

'Oh, no, he isn't,' she said from the heart.

Josh looked alarmed.

'But you're *friends*.'

Izzy looked at the lazy predatory animal that was Dominic Templeton-Burke. 'I very much doubt it,' she said grimly.

Jemima had put on a lot of sophistication in the last few months, but she wasn't in the tiger class yet. Not in her friendships, thought Izzy. Lovers, yes—Izzy could believe that. Newly dazzled by success, Jemima was quite capable of falling in love with a lord of the universe. But being his friend? No.

And Dominic Templeton-Burke did not look like the sort of man to settle for friendship with a gorgeous girl like Jemima either. So were she and this prowling sophisticate lovers?

I must have been mad.

She gave herself a mental shake. This was no time to lose her nerve! *You make your own luck.* That was what she always said to Jemima. So here was where she practised what she preached.

She swallowed hard and glared past Josh's right shoulder straight into the mirrors where Dominic Templeton-Burke's eyes should be.

Josh said worriedly, 'Molly told me they said they had brought him in because you were nervous about the jump. They thought you'd be glad to have him along.'

'Glad!'

Even to her own ears she sounded appalled. Josh looked startled.

Careful, Izzy! Nearly gave yourself away there!

Attack is the best form of defence, Izzy reminded herself. She said disagreeably, 'Why is he dressed up like Rambo?'

And, of course, she said it just as Nightmare Man came within earshot. He stopped dead, and suddenly he was not so lazy any more. He stiffened, and the mirrored glasses trained on her like lasers.

Josh looked uneasy. 'Who knows?' he muttered, half under his breath. 'They all say Dom is a law unto himself.'

'Really?' Izzy was back in her part now, the super-cool model-girl who never let anything throw her. She narrowed her eyes at the powerful figure and said deliberately, 'That makes two of us.'

And stepped out of the limo like a queen.

'Don't antagonise him,' besought Josh in an anguished undervoice. 'You've no idea how hard we had to work to get him here. If you rub him up the wrong way he could walk. He doesn't care what anybody thinks.'

She could believe it. The man had stopped and was just standing there, arms across his chest, unashamedly enjoying the view exposed by her flimsy floaty top.

Sexist pig, thought Izzy, wanting to hit him.

She didn't. But she did tip her chin ever so slightly higher. And straighten, locking gazes with him.

She held her breath. This was the point at which he fell back crying, *This woman is an impostor,* and every photographer there closed in for the kill. She felt sick again. At once, Izzy reminded herself she'd faced things a whole lot worse than that and glared right into the masking sunglasses.

The man seemed to freeze.

Oh, God, here it comes, she thought.

It was difficult to tell, with those mirrored sunglasses masking his eyes, but she thought he was shocked. Swallowing, she braced herself...

And then, suddenly, the prowling predator turned human. He grinned, and two deep clefts appeared in his thin face.

'Second thoughts?' he said by way of greeting.

Izzy could not believe it. Not a word about, *Who is this woman?* or *Where is Jemima?* He sounded as if he thought her hostility was funny. Yet for some reason his voice wound the tension knots in her stomach even tighter.

'If you're asking whether I've lost my nerve,' she snapped, 'the answer is no.'

At once she was ashamed of herself. Nearly apologised, even. Then thought, No, model girls are allowed to be brattish. It was probably just what Josh and the tiger were expecting.

'No?'

Dominic looked at his watch ostentatiously. It was a big thing, full of dials, and it glinted in the sun. But it was not his watch that Izzy was staring at.

It was his forearm, tanned and sinewy. He looked *strong*. Izzy swallowed. Not all strong, physical men are bullies, she told herself rapidly. You can't judge every man in combat gear by one bad experience.

So— 'No,' she said fiercely, as much to herself as to him. 'I never lose my nerve.'

'I believe you.' His tone said the reverse.

She could have danced with rage. 'Never,' she insisted.

He shrugged. 'Then hurry up and weigh in and let's get this show on the road.'

Izzy was taken aback. 'Weigh in?'

'Weight is important. That's how they work out which bungee rope to use.'

She was instantly wary. 'No one told me I'd have to be weighed.'

Dominic Templeton-Burke looked sardonic. 'It's painless.'

'But—'

Josh misinterpreted her. 'It's okay. They're not allowed to tell anyone else,' he said reassuringly. 'That's in the contract.'

Dominic gave a snort of laughter. Izzy was disliking him more by the minute. And not just because of his choice of wardrobe.

'There's no need to snigger,' she told him. 'I'm trying to be professional here.'

He shrugged again, bored. 'And your weight is a professional secret?'

That was a new thought. Izzy paused, momentarily uncertain. She would certainly be heavier that Jemima. Did the tabloids know what her sister weighed? Would the discrepancy give her away? Izzy could have groaned aloud.

But she didn't. Instead, she decided to go on a charm offensive. She pushed back the soft red hair that smelled of Jemima's conditioner and gave Dominic Templeton-Burke the best smile she could muster. Too little, too late, of course, but at least she could try.

'No woman wants to broadcast her weight,' she said, trying to sound conciliating.

He was not conciliated. 'Whatever. Are we doing this jump or not?'

Not if I had a choice. I want to run away from you and your masked eyes and your horrible muscular arms and...

But she couldn't. There was too much riding on this. Oh, not her pride. Her pride had taken a beating before and recovered. But there was Jemima to think about. So running wasn't an option. She had no choice. She had to stick it out.

Just because he looked strong and dressed like a jungle fighter, that was no reason to be afraid of the man, Izzy told herself firmly. In fact, the exact opposite, she thought, warming to her theme. Who but a complete pillock needed camouflage gear on the South Bank of the Thames at eleven o'clock on a bright sunny morning?

He was just playing at being a soldier. And not even a real soldier, a Hollywood version, straight from Central Casting. It was pathetic!

Yes, that made her feel a lot better.

Dominic Templeton-Burke stayed in role, though. 'Coming?' he asked. It was—nearly—a taunt.

Izzy's chin went so high it was almost vertical. 'Of course,' she said, not bothering to conciliate any more.

'Then let's go.'

CHAPTER FIVE

DOMINIC could not believe it. *It was her.*

His heart gave a great leap. At last—his lady in red!

He had found her! Just as he was beginning to think that his careful strategy had failed. Just as he was accepting that he would to have to ask spiky Molly di Peretti for the name of the woman she called Management but who was not—as his Internet researches had already established—Pepper Calhoun. Just as his patience was stretched to breaking point and his temper balanced on a knife edge. Suddenly, the wheel of chance spun again. His luck changed. And here she was.

Only— 'Let's go,' she said. *Let's go!* As if they had never met before. As if she had never melted into his arms as if she belonged there. As if she had never danced around him until their bodies pulsed to the same beat. Or driven his heart into a wild fandango.

He tried to make her meet his eyes. *Look at me,* he said to her silently, fiercely. Once she looked into his eyes she would have to give up pretending. She would have to acknowledge what was between them. Acknowledge *him*.

But it was no good. She appeared to be glaring straight at him, but she wasn't. She was glaring at a Dominic-shaped space. And she looked as if she were spitting mad.

That was when his head caught up with his hormones.

What is going on here?

Behind her the lad from Culp and Christopher—what was his name? Josh?—said, 'You and Dom go ahead. I'll wait out here, Jemima.'

Dom stopped dead. Jemima?

Jemima?

His lady in red was never Jemima Dare! He *knew* Jemima Dare. He had danced with her in a desultory fashion at a charity ball in the winter. Or rather he had propped her up on her impossibly high heels while she waggled her head in time to the music. No abandoned dancer, she! And she had never made his heart skip a beat, much less go into that wild fandango.

This woman was not Jemima Dare. She had not been Jemima Dare when she drove him mad on that nightclub dance floor. And she was not Jemima Dare now.

Except…

People changed. He knew that. She had Jemima Dare's height. She had the same pale, perfect skin. Okay, women changed their hair at the touch of a bottle, but she seemed to be another spectacular redhead. *Could* she have been Jemima Dare all along? Reinvented by the night and the music into a new woman before turning back into a dull celebrity at midnight?

Dom swung round, staring at her.

'No!' he said aloud, appalled.

She did not hear him. Or she didn't want to hear him. Instead, she motioned him to lead the way into the wooden shack that served as an office, as if she had blanked their frantic embraces out of her memory.

Dom was outraged. They'd sent each other up in flames. She *had* to remember.

But they had reached the office and he saw, suddenly, just how nervous she was. Oh, she waved brightly enough to the photographers. But she was nervous.

Why? She was beautiful. Far more beautiful than the skinny kid in her glitter frock at the ball in February. She had curves, wonderful curves that he could sketch from memory. It wasn't just her looks, either. This woman might not look at him but he could feel the turmoil inside her. She was a real bonfire of physical responses.

Now she sent Dom a defiant look as she stepped on the scales. She did not even glance at the figure as the efficient woman in charge wrote it in indelible marker on the back of her hand.

Dom was convinced. No professional model ever showed that lack of interest in her weight! He had partied with enough of them to know. Whoever she was, his lady in red was not Jemima Dare. His instincts were right, after all.

Suddenly his lips twitched.

'You live an interesting life,' he told her.

The woman who was *not* Jemima Dare glared at him suspiciously.

'What?'

'Infinite variety,' he said smoothly. 'From scented catwalk to a crane over the river.' He paused. Then added softly, 'With lots of bad behaviour in the back of taxis in between, no doubt.'

Disappointingly, she did not rise to that. 'These days I'm strictly limousine class,' she said with satisfaction.

He decided to probe a little. 'No bad behaviour at all?'

She gave a short bark of laughter that disconcerted him. 'Definitely not. I've always been the good girl. It's my sister Izzy who does the bad stuff. Always has.'

'She sounds like fun,' he said politely, bored. 'And you never kick your heels up at all?'

Her mouth tightened. 'What makes you think I would discuss it with you, even if I did?' She sent him a dark look. 'Don't you ever take those damned sunglasses off? They make you look like a total nerd. You can't possibly need them in here!'

He whipped them off. 'Absolutely.'

It took the wind out of her sails completely. Her head went back and her eyes narrowed as if he had taken up a challenge and she did not quite know what to do about it. He enjoyed that.

He also enjoyed saying in a kind voice, 'Better concentrate on what she's showing you. The safety harness is important, you know.'

She did not answer. But she made a sound under her breath that sounded like 'Grrr.'

Dominic bit back a smile and instantly went into Best Pupil in the Class mode. For the first time in his life. Well, he tried. The woman who wasn't Jemima was just too fascinating for him to concentrate on Sandy's spiel about drag co-efficients. Especially as he knew most of it already.

Their instructress was clear and concise. She took them both through the buckles and failsafes of the harness. Then she outlined the safety procedures.

'They'll go through it again before you jump; don't worry. Now, just a few questions about your present state of health.'

Izzy listened with gratitude. She kept trying to tell herself that Dominic Templeton-Burke was just a wannabe Hollywood hero and totally pathetic, but it wasn't working. He didn't *feel* pathetic. He felt like a powerhouse. And he was studying her as if she were a specimen under a microscope. She could feel her heart rate bouncing around all over the place under that too close inspection.

'Stop looking at me and pay attention,' she told him sharply. 'This isn't a game. It's only sensible to know about the risks.'

His eyebrows flew up. She thought his lips twitched, too. Damn him, he was *laughing* at her.

Izzy turned her shoulder and paid ostentatious attention to the rest of the talk. And then she answered their questions with care as she ran her eye down the list they gave her.

'No—no damage to my spinal column,' she said, ticking the box. 'My blood pressure's normal.'

Well, it would be if Dominic Templeton-Burke weren't standing so close that she could feel his breath skittering over Jemima's hairspray to find the sensitive spot just below her ear.

'No—no heart condition, no epilepsy. No, I'm not pregnant.'

A noise—no, not a noise, a slight shifting of the air—made her look up. It was Dominic Templeton-Burke, twice as sardonic now that he had removed his sunglasses. His eyes were limpid grey with little flecks of green. They met hers with undisguised amusement.

'Don't be silly, Sandy,' he said to the efficient woman, though he was looking straight at Izzy. 'Model girls at the height of their earning power don't get pregnant. Bad for business.'

Izzy choked. It was only by a great effort of will that she kept the professionally indifferent mask in place.

'You know so much about models, of course?' she enquired with spurious politeness.

'Doesn't everyone?'

'You don't know anything at all about me,' she flashed. It was out before she had time to reconsider. And, in the circumstances, it was probably a mistake.

He laughed aloud. 'Don't tell me! You've become a Buddhist since the last time I had my hands on you. And now you only care about things of the spirit.'

Their eyes locked: his quizzical, hers stunned.

'The last time you had your hands on me?' echoed Izzy. Her voice was hollow.

He struck an attitude. 'You've forgotten,' he said dramatically.

Izzy felt sick. Oh, God, he and Jemima *must* have been lovers. How was she going to busk her way through this one?

But she had prepared for this, she reminded herself. Or something like it. She had known there was bound to be a chance that she would bump into someone who was a risk to the deception. Okay, her preparation had not starred Tall, Dark and Handsome from the Marines. And she had not bargained on an ex-lover, either. But she could deal with anyone she had to, including him. Heck, he couldn't read her mind. And so far he hadn't noticed that she was not Jemima either.

Hang on to that, Izzy.

She pulled herself together. 'I forget a lot of men,' she said coolly.

The nice woman who had explained the safety procedures gave a crack of laughter. Clearly she knew Dominic Templeton-Burke rather well. Maybe another of his ex-lovers, thought Izzy sourly.

'One in the eye for you, Dom,' said the nice woman cheerfully.

He laughed. Well, he had to, didn't he? But the look he gave Izzy was thoughtful.

Izzy pretended not to notice. If his ego couldn't take it—tough! She ignored him pointedly. 'Is that all?'

The woman pushed a form at her. 'Sign here. Then we'll get you both into the harness and take you up.'

Izzy signed. Dominic Templeton-Burke still did not take his eyes off her. She could feel his gaze, even though she did not look at him.

Oh, Lord, this was bad. Was there unfinished business between him and Jemima? Something, certainly. Some argument that he had taken personally? He was looking at her as narrowly as a police witness trying to pick a criminal out of a line up.

Could things get any worse?

Izzy swallowed hard. She had to get his gaze off her face. It was just too keen, too alert.

Flirtatiously, she shook back her long shining red hair. She had never felt less flirtatious in her life. But the hair was what people remembered. It was like a cape of shimmering silk, an unbelievable colour, unbelievably soft. It was the hair of a Renaissance beauty.

Izzy knew that. She had read the press files. This morning it gleamed in the sun like flame, like wine. This morning it almost looked like Jemima's instead of ratty old Izzy's red mop.

She had worked hard on the hair. She was proud of it. If he could be distracted by the hair he might not notice that she was too tall, too heavy and too freckled to be Jemima.

'Okay. I'm ready,' she said, feeling the hair float about her bare shoulders.

He *had* to be looking at her hair.

He was. He came right up behind her. She felt his hand on the back of her waist. Then her nape. He was gathering up her hair in one hand. She thought she could feel his breath on the exposed skin. Did his hand linger?

Oh, yes, she had distracted him all right.

Through a mist of unwelcome sensation, Izzy tried hard to congratulate herself. It was a good strategy, she told herself feverishly. As long as he was looking at her through a fog of lust he wasn't going to start making comparisons and uncover her secret.

The trouble was, it had its drawbacks. The fog of lust seemed to be travelling. It wasn't just Dominic who was being distracted. Unexpectedly, she gave a little shiver of pure physical sensation.

Damn!

Dominic Templeton-Burke said in a cool voice, 'I suggest you plait this. If it gets caught on the harness it will really make your eyes water.'

Izzy could have screamed. She twitched her hair out of his grasp and stepped away.

'Thank you,' she said arctically. But her body was not arctic. Not arctic at all.

Somewhere in the normal world, nice Sandy was agreeing with him. 'Good point, Dom. Do you want an elastic band, Ms Dare?'

Dom gave another of those snorts of private laughter. He obviously thought that model-girl hair needed a lot more pampering than a simple elastic band. For some reason that made her want to dance and scream with frustration. How dared he patronise her—well, Jemima—no, both of them—like that?

Dislike was altogether too mild a word. Izzy decided she hated him.

She gritted her teeth and decided to focus on practical matters instead of the alluring prospect of pushing Dominic Templeton-Burke into the river.

'That's okay, thanks,' she told Sandy curtly. 'I can handle it.'

She had some of her own long pins in her bag. Jemima wouldn't use them at any price. She said they broke the hair. But Izzy always used them whenever she put her hair up. Now she twisted the shining mass into a rapid rope and pinned it in place with a couple of savage jabs.

All the time, Dom watched her unwinkingly. She knew it. She could *feel* it, even when she wasn't actually looking at him.

He said casually, 'How long have you supported the one-parent whale?'

Izzy nearly dropped a pin. 'What?'

His smile widened. Not pleasantly. 'You don't even know what charity this is for, do you?'

She could not deny it.

He said suddenly, 'What's happened to you, Jemmy?'

Jemmy? *Jemmy?* Nobody called her sister Jemmy. Was it a private name? Lover's code for, *I love you, you're mine, nobody knows you like I do?*

Izzy went cold. Oh God, it was true! They *had* to be lovers. Well, have been lovers. Jemima had been travelling too much these last few months for any relationship to survive.

How long had it been going on? And why on earth had her sister not told her? A little chill of sadness struck. How well did she know Jemima these days, after all?

She stopped fussing with her hair and stared at him, frowning.

He shook his head. 'I don't remember you being this hungry for publicity, babe.' And he touched her cheek fleetingly.

Fleetingly, but it might as well have been a bolt of lightning. Izzy's breath caught in her throat. For a wild moment she thought, I can't breathe!

And then, Is that he does to Jemima? Does he make her stop breathing, too? And does he know? And, if so, who broke up with whom? And how does he feel about it? Does he want to throw me off that crane for revenge?

And then, What if I've got it wrong and they haven't broken up?

He-el—lp!

Dominic gave her an easy smile. 'Hey, don't look like that, babe. What's the worst that can happen?'

Izzy moistened her suddenly dry lips. 'I don't know,' she said with feeling. 'You tell me.'

He obviously thought it was the height that bothered her.

'You scream. I carry you back to earth. We both get our pictures in the paper.' He sounded infuriatingly unperturbed by this scenario.

Izzy pulled herself together. 'And then I die of shame,' she retorted. 'Oh, well, I suppose I can always run away to sea.'

'Practical,' he said approvingly.

It was on the tip of her tongue to say, I'm always practical, but she reined it in just in time. Because if he and Jemima were ex-lovers, he must know that, spectacular, charming and sexy as she undoubtedly was, Jemima Dare was the ditziest woman in England. Or he would if he had ever bothered to think about her. But maybe he didn't. Maybe it was all lust for Jemima the gorgeous siren, and he didn't care what she was like inside.

Let's hope so, thought Izzy, setting her teeth.

'Let's go jump,' she said curtly.

They were each weighed again; the harness was attached and tested briefly. Dominic ran the rope through his hands, tugging it professionally in various directions. As the cage creaked and swayed up the crane to the jump point he inspected the buckles of the harness with meticulous care.

Then he shocked Izzy into rigidity by putting his arm round her.

'Oh!' she exclaimed, as if he had stabbed her.

He looked down at her, mildly surprised.

She knew why, too. It was not a sexual touch. Barely even a friendly one. It was as clinical as if he were testing her dimensions to ship her across a ravine. But she still recoiled like a wounded duellist.

'Hey. Relax.'

'I'm relaxed. I'm relaxed,' muttered Izzy with determination. She tried to tell herself that it was true. But she stood under his hands as stiff as the scaffolding that surrounded them.

Dominic was clearly amused. 'You're going to have to hang onto me when we jump. You might just as well start now.'

That shook her out of her frozen awareness. 'What?'

He looked down at her, the grey eyes glinting devilishly. 'That's the point of jumping together. Didn't they explain that?'

'N-no.'

His eyes danced. 'Someone has blundered,' he said in mock outrage.

'You can say that again.'

'We can always turn round and go back down again. Want to?'

It was a temptation. Oh, boy, was it a temptation. But Izzy knew what would happen if she chickened out now. Instead of the few column inches in obscure corners of tomorrow's papers, she'd get some serious publicity. She could just see the headlines: 'Missing Model Seeks Treatment'. Jemima needed that like she needed a hole in her head.

Just a few more hours, she told herself. *Just finish this and it's over. You're a free woman by lunchtime.*

She swallowed. 'No. Now we're on the way I'll do whatever it takes.'

'Good girl,' he said, surprising her.

The cage lurched to a halt and he ushered her out onto the jump platform. The other people up there were pleasant but preoccupied. They talked to Dom as an equal. But to her they were kind and faintly patronising. Izzy had the sensation of being an unimportant piece of baggage in the middle of a professional operation.

She hugged her arms round herself. The morning was bright with sunshine but it was all she could do not to start shivering uncontrollably. And it was nothing to do with the height of the platform, although below them the Thames looked like a river on a toy farm. It was the thought of being held by Dominic Templeton-Burke as they launched themselves into space.

Izzy watched covertly as he discussed winds and air pressure. He was gorgeous. He was a danger to Jemima. He was her nightmare.

And he made her tremble like a schoolgirl.

Great! The one man in the world she had to play like a professional was turning out to be the one man in the world she wasn't sure she could deal with. And already he was suspicious, she knew.

Oh, well, she would have to try to pretend it was all sex and astonishment. Maybe he would buy that. And she'd have to get away from him after the jump with the speed of Superman.

He stepped back from the edge. 'Ready?'

Izzy remembered why they were there and her stomach lurched. *No.*

She clenched her teeth until her jaw ached. 'Yes,' she said aloud.

He threw his arms wide. 'Then come into my arms.'

Izzy gave a snort of pure exasperation. 'Oh, pu-lease!'

His eyes laughed at her. 'This is no time to turn skittish on me, my love.'

She couldn't help herself. Those jumpy instincts of hers! 'I'm not your love,' she said, before she could stop herself.

He chuckled. 'Yes, you are. For the day, anyway. The guys down there are waiting for the full airborne embrace.'

The trouble was, she knew he was right. On the riverbank below them the photographers were focussing their zoom lenses for all they were worth. It did not make her like Dominic Templeton-Burke any more, but she knew her duty. She pulled herself together and managed a wide, false smile.

'You're so romantic,' she told him sarcastically.

She waved jauntily at the watchers, hundreds of feet below. And stepped into his embrace.

For a moment she was shockingly aware of the heat of his body, the beat of blood—his, hers— the odd jingle of the harness, voices, hands... As if it was all happening to someone else, she listened to the last repeat of the instructions, nodded her understanding, did what she was told.

Tried not to shake.

'You wanted poetry. Come to the edge,' Dom said, with a ghost of a laugh.

Poetry. *Poetry?* His hands were warm on her shoulderblades.

Memory flickered. 'What are you talking about?' said Izzy, suspiciously.

'You know. If you think about it.'

Oh, God, this was more of that secret lovers' language! Izzy was so wretched that she nearly fell off that precarious platform without waiting for the instruction to go. She did not actually miss her footing, but for a moment her head swam and she clutched at him in pure reflex.

So much for her determination not to get too close! It made her groan.

'This is one crazy day.'

'And it's only just started,' he said in congratulatory tones.

Izzy's stomach lurched. She was not afraid of heights, or the bungee jump. But just the thought of spending one more moment with Dominic than was strictly necessary turned her blood to ice.

'Oh, help!'

He misunderstood. He laughed, not unkindly.

'It's not as bad as it looks.'

'You have no idea,' said Izzy unwarily.

His hands moved on her back. Was he *stroking* her?

His voice was odiously reassuring. 'Stick with me; I'll see you through. Trust me.'

Izzy had no option. She had to look at the laughing renegade six inches from her nose. Her heart did a back flip and sank to her sequinned trainers. Idiot, idiot, *idiot*, she thought, for the twentieth time that day.

Aloud she said, 'I can't do it.'

It was pure panic. She made no attempt to hide it. What was the point?

The renegade laughed. 'I can.'

Izzy moaned.

He held her closer. 'Think about one-parent whales. That ought to do it.'

Izzy stopped moaning. She pushed herself back in his embrace and glared up at him. 'Thank you very much for your support.'

He laughed, not quite so kindly. 'You got yourself into this. I'll get you out of it—but at a price.'

'A price?'

'We'll talk about that later. For now, just close your eyes and trust me.'

Izzy swallowed. 'Do I have a choice?'

He shook his head. He was laughing but oh, boy, that determination!

'Come fly with me,' said Dominic Templeton-Burke, grinning.

Izzy shuddered.

'And afterwards I'll buy you a hamburger and we can discuss poets.'

Izzy decided that she was going to hate him for the rest of her life, without any difficulty at all. But she was not going to let him see how feeble she felt inside. Not any more.

She squinted up at him and plastered on a bright, bright smile.

'I look forward to it,' she said, planning her getaway the moment she hit the ground.

'Then let's do this thing.'

They stepped to the edge of the platform in careful concurrence. His arms about her were hard. They felt stronger than any harness.

Startled, Izzy thought, *He will keep me safe.*
He said, 'Now.'
She said, 'No, not yet. Let me—'
But he moved. She was locked to his body.
He said urgently, 'Don't think about the drop.
Think about me.'
He kissed her hard.
And the bottom fell out of the world.

CHAPTER SIX

TOGETHER, they were shooting down, down, down...

This is where I'm supposed to scream, thought Izzy. But his mouth cut off all sound; damn nearly all thought.

Okay, in his combats and shades he was the man out of her every nightmare. But she knew this kiss, these arms. He was the man from her night of fantasy as well.

How could she ever have wondered whether he was real? What figment of imagination had muscles like that? Kissed like this?

He was real. He was a danger. He was almost certainly Jemima's.

But just for the moment he was all hers and he kissed like a dream. Even in mid air, while they bounced like a pair of delinquent babies, her whole being responded to that kiss.

Oh, wow. Oh, hell. Oh, *heaven.*

'That was great,' enthused Josh when they got to the ground again.

Izzy didn't say anything. Her legs felt as if they

did not belong to her and she suspected that she was white as a sheet. She just hoped they would put it down to reaction to the jump.

'Terrific shot,' agreed one of the photographers. He looked from her to Dominic speculatively. 'Know each other well?'

Izzy swallowed, and was almost grateful when Dominic fielded it neatly.

'We do now,' he said with a grin.

But the enquirer was persistent. 'You're close?'

'You couldn't get a paperclip between us,' said Dominic solemnly.

A couple of the photographers chuckled but the questioner was not deflected.

'Come on—give. You guys an item now?'

Dominic put an arm round her shoulders. Izzy twitched. But the pressure was a warning rather than imminent seduction, and she knew it. She stayed quiet. It was out of character. But it seemed to be her day for behaving out of character, thought Izzy.

Day? Make that fortnight! She hadn't picked up a man on the dance floor since she was a teenager. Oh, she pulled, right enough. People did. You had a dance, a drink, maybe a chat with his friends and hers. You exchanged phone numbers. You checked each other out. And if the attraction was still there the next day, and he wasn't a creep, you went out with him.

She had *never* gone home with a total stranger. Oh, yes, this was her time for going out of character all right!

Dominic was saying easily, 'You know me and girlfriends! It would be nice to get that lucky.'

There was a comradely laugh. Someone shouted a friendly encouragement. Dominic kept his arm right where it was and squeezed. It must have looked like the last word in casual, sexy sophistication.

Izzy gritted her teeth and smiled for the camera. But inside she felt hollow. I'm not sexy, I'm not sophisticated and I sure as hell am not casual, she thought. What on earth am I going to do about this?

He gave her another friendly squeeze. 'Come on, kid. Let's get the harness off.'

She nodded. She even managed a friendly wave as she followed Dominic into the hut. Nobody would be able to tell that she was still cold with shock, she thought. Not even Dominic.

She shook back her hair with a bright smile. Hey, she could act a whole lot better than she'd ever realised, thought Izzy. She tried to take comfort from her unsuspected acting skills. But even that didn't really penetrate the force field of shock that surrounded her.

In the hut, she fumbled with the harness and could not move it.

'I'm all thumbs,' she said, disgusted with herself.

'Disorientation,' said Dominic. 'You haven't got your dry land legs back yet.'

He strolled over and dealt swiftly with canvas straps and buckles.

'Thank you,' said Izzy, struggling not to sound stifled.

He was so close! She caught the whiff of sandalwood. Her head went back as if she had walked into a wall. That smell! It pierced the protective force field and flicked open a memory file.

In the taxi... She had rubbed her face against his wrist. He'd had a chunky watch with all sorts of dials on it. He'd thought she was wonderful...

He was unbuckling the final restraint from her waist. But suddenly he looked up, as if she had said something.

At once Izzy was not hollow and shocked any more. She was hot as fire.

She just stood there, looking down at him. His eyes were so calm, clear as grey lake water, with those little flecks of green in their depths. Calm and compelling and sexy as hell. And they seemed to slide right into her core.

Suddenly Izzy couldn't think. Couldn't breathe. She put a hand to her throat but she could not tear her eyes away.

Dominic smiled. Slowly.

He stood up.

Izzy stood rooted to the spot. There were other people in the shack but she and Dominic Templeton-Burke could have been alone on the moon for all the notice she took of them. He put his hand on her shoulder. Her lips parted…

And Josh from Culp and Christopher breezed in and said, 'Ready to go, Jemima?'

Dominic swung round and stopped him by dint of stepping in his path and putting a hand in the middle of his chest.

Like a traffic policeman, thought Izzy. She nearly laughed aloud. I must be light-headed, she thought. All that bouncing upside down on the end of a line has scrambled my brains!

'It's okay,' Dominic said. 'I'll take it from here.'

Josh goggled. 'But the limo—I've got to see Jemima back to her hotel.'

Izzy opened her mouth to protest but Dominic said swiftly, 'Been a change of plan.'

'They didn't tell me,' said Josh, martyred. 'Typical.'

'Spur of the moment,' said Dominic truthfully. 'We're having lunch where the photographers won't find us.' And he winked heavily.

'Oh,' said Josh enlightened. 'Well—if it's like that—do you want the limo?'

Dom shook his head. 'Take it away with you. I'll get her home safe.' He managed an avuncular smile that made Izzy want to laugh even louder.

'No doubt about that,' said Josh, laughing heartily. 'With a sister in the firm, you're practically one of us.'

Izzy came out of her cocoon. 'I don't want lunch, thank you.'

Dom sent her a twinkling look. 'You may not. But are you going to deny the baying hordes the shot they're waiting for?'

'Which shot is that?' said Izzy suspiciously.

'You and me driving off into the sunset. Well, lunchtime Battersea anyway.'

Josh was impressed. 'Good point.'

Izzy was outraged. 'Driving off into the sunset?'

'You heard them. Are Jemima Dare and me an item? That's what they want to know.'

Them and me both, thought Izzy. She decided to take a risk. 'So tell them we're not.'

He laughed gently. 'You sure about that?'

Their eyes locked.

'I'll just say goodbye to the charity people,' Izzy said curtly.

She banged out of the cabin. Everyone else followed her, like a royal entourage.

Left alone, Dominic shook his head. This was going to take careful handling.

She was keeping her powder dry for the moment. But he did not think that Not-Jemima was going to co-operate for much longer. He wondered if she would risk going to head with head him in an all-out battle in front of this interested audience. His best guess was that the odds were even.

Gosh, this was going to be fun!

Outside, she was talking to a couple of the charity organisers. They had given her a tee shirt and a certificate and she swung this way and that, holding the things up to display them both for the cameras. She looked, thought Dom, happier than she had been all morning. She was even laughing.

When she laughed, she was spectacular. Something that was not amusement turned over in his gut.

How on earth did she think she could get away with impersonating that milk-and-water kid he had met in February? And how on earth did the idiot boy from Culp and Christopher not see the difference?

Oh, the hair was the same, he supposed. Come to think of it, so were the camellia-pale skin and the slanting eyes, the cheekbones. But this woman sizzled. No comparison at all.

But then Josh had presumably not seen her dancing like a wild thing in that murky club. Or held her in his arms while she burbled about poetry and turned his blood to a roar. Or put her to bed like a gentleman when she passed out cold. Josh had no unfinished business with her.

Dom shook his head wryly. Even so—if he was the only person who saw that she was an impostor, then the whole damned world was mad. And very soon she was going to tell him why.

Meanwhile, the only thing to do was kick back and enjoy it. He propped his shoulder against the doorjamb and watched, smiling.

To begin with she had looked like any other laminated doll in her silly clothes. But now, after her jump, hair mussed and eyes sparkling, she had turned human suddenly—human and deeply alluring. That slightly rumpled look made any red-blooded man want to rumple her a whole lot more. From the way they were clicking furiously, even the photographers could see it.

'She's wearing all the wrong gear,' complained Josh, coming up beside him. 'C&C gave me a list, and one of the journos has been telling me that she's changed it all round. Down to her underwear.'

Dom was startled. 'Her underwear? How do they know that?'

'Er—shape,' said Josh, gloomily depressed. 'She's got more than they were expecting, apparently.' He looked across at her. 'She is just so gorgeous.' There was an odd note in his voice.

Dom flicked up an eyebrow. 'You sound surprised.'

'Well, she always looks good. But today she's special.'

Dom pursed his lips. 'She certainly doesn't look like her photographs,' he said, testing the ground cautiously.

'They never do. What isn't make-up is air brushing. The real person is always smaller and thinner. But today there *is* something different about her.'

'Terror?' suggested Dom.

Josh laughed. 'That has to be it.'

Time to get rid of the competition. 'And me being here, too, maybe. She wasn't expecting that. Look, Josh, I wasn't joking about taking her off to lunch.' He gave him a frank man-to-man look. 'We've got things to catch up on.'

'Oh,' said Josh. 'But—she didn't seem too keen.'

'A *lot* of things to catch up on.'

'Ah,' said Josh, a man of the world. 'Right you are, then. I'll take the limo and slip away now.'

Dom thumped him between the shoulderblades. 'Good man. I owe you.'

He watched Josh disappear through the gates and curbed the desire to laugh aloud.

'God, I'm good,' he muttered.

Across the tarmac, Not-Jemima was laughing at something one of the old guys from the charity had said. Not serious competition, but a distraction they could both do without, he thought.

Time to tell her Josh had gone and left her to Dom's care. She wouldn't be pleased, he thought, amused. Interesting to see how much of a fuss she was willing to make in public. She was working very hard to keep her reaction to him under deep, deep cover. Not doing too bad a job at all, either.

Time to test it a little. Go for it, Dom!

He strolled over and lowered his voice to that intimate growl that always got results. 'Ready to go, babe?'

It got a reaction all right. She couldn't have heard him coming because she leaped about a foot in the air and spun round, as if he had fired a pistol. Oh, she got hold of herself fast enough. But the brown eyes stayed wary—and more than wary.

He wondered what she would do if he said casually, How much do you remember of the night I put you to bed?

It was a sore temptation. But not fair, with all those photographers and charity workers and PR people around. Congratulating himself on his chivalry, Dom put the subject on hold. For the moment.

She said in a neutral voice, 'There's no need—'

He gave her one of the wide, friendly smiles he used on suspicious headmen who didn't want him tracking through their territory. 'It's the least I can do after you were so brave up there.' He smiled round at the others. 'I had to promise her a hamburger to get her to jump.'

There was a general laugh. After a moment, Not-Jemima joined in. Dom could see the effort it cost her. He wondered if anyone else did.

She said, 'I'm fine now. No hamburger necessary.'

'But I want to,' said Dom gently.

Their eyes met like a clash of light sabres. No question about it. She wanted to get away from him as fast as she decently could.

Well, she could try. This was a chess game. He was good at chess. He waited enjoyably.

There was a pause. Then, 'I can't go to just any old burger joint. The fans are impossible.'

It sounded vain and pettish, and he ought to have despised her for it. But somehow Dom knew she didn't mean it. Well, she *meant* it. He had never known a woman struggle so hard not to have a meal with him. But the vanity was pure camouflage.

It would spike her guns if he played along.

Soothingly he said, 'I'll take you to a place where we can keep the fans at bay, I promise.'

'Josh is waiting for me—'

'Josh has gone. I told him,' said Dom, 'that we had a lot to catch up on.'

Her chin came up dangerously. 'I see.'

He'd been right about that, then. She was a cool customer, all right.

She unpinned the glorious red hair and let it flow round her bare shoulders, fluffing it out with her fingers after its confinement. It was a very model-girl gesture, he thought, amused.

'Agreed?' He let his voice take on a caressing note.

She nodded slowly. 'Agreed.'

She gave him a wide, photogenic smile, but he could see that behind the smile she was bracing herself. Nobody else picked it up; he was certain. But to Dom it came across as loud and clear as if she had it spelled out on the tee shirt, instead of the Alzheimer's research charity logo.

He did not like that. He was perfectly willing to duel with her as long as she wanted. But he hated the thought of Not-Jemima bracing herself to spend time with him.

He said, more crisply than he'd intended, 'Shall we go then?'

She shrugged. But she made her farewells and let him lead her to his four-wheel drive. He had spent several days working on it and the engine was honed to perfection. But the bodywork still bore the traces of its last expedition down through the Essex salt flats. It was streaked with dried mud and enough dust to start a new desert all on its own.

The expression on her face was not hard to interpret. The Culp and Christopher limo she'd arrived in had gleamed like a Guards' officer's riding boots.

'Not up to your standards of luxury,' he said, entertained. He held the door open for her.

She climbed in, ignoring the helping hand he offered.

'Not at all,' she said calmly. She looked down at him, her eyes deceptively innocent. 'Just surprised. I mean, it's just not a very ecologically sound car for town driving, is it? I thought an explorer would be keener on the environment than that.'

He blinked, utterly taken aback.

'You don't think I'm green enough?' he said, stunned.

She allowed herself a small smile.

It delighted him. 'You're winding me up,' he said on a note of discovery.

She was airy. 'Just telling it like it is.'

He went round the other side and swung up into the driver's seat.

'Then let me put this thing in context.' He started the engine. 'I don't live in London—just hole up in the family flat once in a while. I have a four-wheel drive because most of my driving is off road. I've had this one for eight years and taken it halfway round the world. And it's in top condition because I service it myself. No evil exhaust fumes. Maximum recycling.'

She looked sceptical. 'If you say so.'

He was amused. But he was put out, too. He went on the offensive. 'You know, you've changed, Jemima,' he said wickedly.

He put the thing in gear and drove out, past the photographers and the remaining groupies. She waved. A bit half-heartedly, he thought.

'Fans getting you down?' he queried sardonically.

She gave a sharp sigh. 'It feels so phoney.'

That sounded like the truth. He was intrigued. 'And that's a problem?'

She made a funny little movement, as if she just picked up a splinter. Her voice changed, turned glib, as if she had practised this bit of dialogue over and over again. 'You get used to it. And I'm grateful. Without the fans I wouldn't have a career.'

He was driving south, away from the river, winding the big vehicle through narrow streets of Victorian terrace houses. It was skilful driving and it needed all his attention. Not taking his eyes off the road, he said dryly, 'Very touching. And who wrote that heartwarming little speech? Culp and Christopher?'

She drew in a hissing breath. 'You're very cynical.'

'And you're very manufactured.' He permitted himself a rapid sideways glance before looking back at the road again.

She gave a brittle laugh. But he knew she didn't like it.

'What makes you say that?'

'The photographers were complaining to Josh. It sounded like they wanted to know every label you're wearing, down to your knickers.'

She gasped, as if he had outraged her. Then, to his astonished delight, she went off into a peal of laughter. Real laughter this time.

'Oh, God, you are so right,' she said, when she could speak. 'You have no idea how right you are.'

He was taken aback. 'What?'

'It's the biggest debate in the fashion world,' she said. Her voice was serious, but out of the corner of his eye he could see that she was primming her mouth up naughtily. 'Thongs or big knickers? We talk about it all the time.'

'Do you?'

He was fascinated. He didn't believe her for a moment. But it did sound as if she knew what she was talking about. She knew somebody who debated thongs and big knickers, no question. Knew them well, by the sound of it. In fact, he'd just bet that information came from the real Jemima Dare, wherever she was.

'Yup. All the time. It's a defining thing for a girl.'

'It is? How?'

She wriggled in the seat. She was enjoying herself, he could see.

'Wear a thong and you're hip. You're cool. You've got a life. Big knickers and you're a sad sack and it's all over.'

'I suppose I don't have to ask which camp you're in?'

'Not if you don't want your head smacked off.'

He could hear the laughter bubbling away under her voice. He said provocatively, 'I like big knickers. In fact, I like the full lace and ribbon number. Preferably knee-length. Gives a chap something to peel off. Slowly.'

That knocked the laughter out of her.

'Oh.'

Good, he thought. He wondered if she were blushing. It was too awkward an angle to tell but he thought there was a chance, just a chance.

Great, so she was off balance. Time to push her a bit. Ask her a question that would force her out into the open.

He said conversationally, 'When did you last make up your own mind about anything? Or do you like having everything organised by your manager, your PR agency and your stylist?'

There was a tiny pause. But she made a fast recovery. She said levelly, 'You're forgetting the hairdresser.'

Damn! Dom raised his brows. 'You *admit* it?'

'Not much point in denying it, is there?' Her voice sounded stifled, as if she were really upset. 'That's the way models live.'

Double damn. He tried again, but he knew she'd blocked him this time. 'Even top models?'

'The nearer the top, the more stylists and hairdressers and manicurists,' she told him coolly.

He began to wonder whether she played chess, too.

He tensed. They took a bend in the road too fast. At once Dom eased off the accelerator. But not before he had heard her indrawn breath.

'Sorry. Are you all right?' he said, annoyed with himself.

She sniffed. 'Of course I'm all right.

'You don't sound all right.'

'That's because I'm feeling seasick,' she said with asperity. 'This car may be a great ride over the grouse moor. But let me tell you it's not a fun experience for the London passenger.'

'Does it bounce too much for you?' he mocked. 'Too used to limousine springing?'

'The springs are fine. It's the way you graze the wing mirrors of parked cars that worries me.'

He was outraged. He'd apologised for the three-wheel cornering, after all! 'I haven't touched a parked car.'

'Maybe not. But you've missed them by a whisker. The passenger,' she pointed out, 'sees it all.'

'Heaven help me, I've got a back seat driver.'

At once she swung round on him. 'Fine. Stop the car and let me out. I'll make my own way home.' The triumph in her voice was almost palpable.

Definitely a chess player! He was going to have to watch this one. *Great!*

'You're very unflattering,' Dom pointed out, between pique and amusement.

'And you're very perverse,' she exclaimed, exasperation throbbing in her voice. 'Why on earth don't you just let me go on my way?'

He digested this.

In the end he said carefully, 'Four reasons. We're a long way from a tube. You won't get a taxi round here at this time of day. I promised to take you home and I always keep my promises. And I owe you a hamburger.'

And the fifth, he thought, though he wasn't going to tell her yet, was: *I want to take all that rumpled sweetness in my hands and rumple you some more until you scream with pleasure.*

He wondered if she already knew that. Sometimes he thought she did. Sometimes he thought she was totally oblivious. Was she blanking him out deliberately while she pretended to be Jemima? Or had she really wiped him out of her memory?

Well, he was nearly as good at memory retrieval as he was at chess.

She said, 'I let you off your promise.'

'No good. I won't. I keep *every* promise, however small.'

She bit her lip. 'Such perfection! You must be hell to live with.'

'Oh, I wouldn't say so. I don't make many promises.'

Dom swung the Jeep into an even smaller street. He reversed into the tightest possible parking space with negligent ease. He switched off the engine and turned to look at her.

She met his eyes defiantly. She was still wearing more make-up than she needed or he liked. But her hair was slightly tangled, with a hint of riotous curl reasserting itself. It brushed her creamy shoulders in a way that positively demanded audience participation.

What would she do if he gave in to his baser instincts? If he reached out and straightened a gleaming lock that had caught itself up behind her ear? If he ran his fingers through it?

'What are you staring at?'

She might look defiant, but her voice gave her away. It jumped about all over the place. He was clearly making her nervous again.

Dom sighed. He did not straighten the alluring lock of hair. Instead he said, still pretending she was Jemima, 'It's a long time since we sat down across a table. I thought we might have a meal together. Catch up a bit. Chill out.'

'*Another* meal,' she said.

He held his breath. This could be where she said, You and I have never had a meal together. We've danced. And I drove you mad with lust. But we didn't eat.

She didn't.

Dom sucked his teeth. Where next? What would he say if she really were Jemima?

'Do you only allow yourself one go at the lettuce leaf a day?' he mocked, inspired.

'*No,*' she said, almost violently.

'Good. Then you will enjoy this place. The food is great and we can sit outside.'

She looked over her shoulder at him. 'Do you ever take no for an answer?'

'Never—when it's important.'

Dom might be curbing his baser instincts as far as that delinquent lock of hair was concerned, but he was not made of iron. She might not have meant it as a challenge, but that look reminded him that her silly floaty sleeves started halfway down her arms. Her bare shoulders just invited a man to touch. Dom was not the man to resist a challenge like that.

He danced his fingers along her naked skin. The moment was so fleeting that she barely had time to catch her breath. But she jerked as if he had lit a fuse.

Yes!

She could lie as much as she liked, thought Dom, jubilant. There was some level at which the woman couldn't help herself. Her body told the truth, no matter what she did.

He jumped out of the car and grinned back at her.

But she did not grin back. She did not move. She looked stunned.

Slowly she lifted her eyes to meet his. And he was totally unprepared.

This was a game for him. A flirtatious chess game of move and counter move, with sexual awareness its tactic and supremacy its goal.

But Not-Jemima Dare looked as if she was carrying all the burdens of the world on her lightly freckled shoulders. Almost as if, just for a moment, she couldn't bear it.

Dom's grin died.

'What is it?' he said urgently. 'What makes you look like that? *Tell* me.'

But she shook her head, and would not look at him as she walked beside him to the little bistro.

It was set on a little triangle of pedestrianised paving that had obviously once been a village square. The restaurant had put tables on the street, among tubs of bay trees, and Dom chose the most discreetly shaded corner. None of the other early diners took any notice of them.

'See?' he said, trying to lighten the atmosphere. 'No fans. You're safe.'

She responded gallantly, even gave a little choke of laughter. 'Safe? Oh, sure.'

He put down the menu and steepled his fingers. 'That's an interesting attitude you've got there.'

'Really?'

Time to bring their battle out into the open. 'You seem to think I'm some sort of threat to you.'

Her jaw tightened. 'That's crazy.'

'That's what I thought,' agreed Dom affably. 'So I'd be glad if you'd explain it to me.'

She shrugged, looking away. The tension in her face was palpable. He said gently, 'What are you afraid of?'

No answer.

He tried again. 'I don't kiss and tell, if that's what worries you.'

He might as well have hit her. All the colour drained from her face with shocking speed. Suddenly he could see the map of careful cosmetics—cheekbones, eyelids, even a line of shading down the perfect nose. She looked as if she had been stripped to the bone. She looked—he *really* didn't like this—defenceless.

He said sharply, 'Don't look like that.'

He could see that she was making the effort to pull herself together. It was a gallant attempt, but the lingering blankness was still in her eyes.

She said in a subdued voice, 'I'm sorry. That damned jump must have upset me more than I realised.'

He looked at her shrewdly. 'The jump? Or me?'

She tossed the wonderful hair. 'Why should seeing you upset me?' She made a good attempt at sounding scornful. But her eyes were watchful.

Dom met her eyes blandly. 'Only you can answer that.'

She started to play with the cutlery, not looking at him. She seemed to be weighing her words. 'Let me ask you something, then. When you said I'd changed—what exactly did you mean?'

He sighed inwardly. Why wouldn't she tell him the truth? Now they were on their own, with no press and no PR people, why couldn't she just come out and say it?

Jemima Dare has taken off to the Seychelles with a married magician and I'm giving her an alibi. Or, *Jemima Dare has hives and I'm the body double.* Did she think he would give them away?

Well, if she wouldn't tell him now, he was going to raise the stakes.

He said carefully, 'I got the feeling that you really didn't want to jump with me this morning. And I couldn't help remembering—you didn't exactly refuse to come into my arms the last time.'

Her eyes flew up to meet his. She looked appalled. 'What?

'Very flattering it was,' he said, his mouth tilting mischievously. 'Had you all over me all evening.'

That was sort of half true. Jemima had been nervous at the big reception and he had been carelessly kind. They'd danced a lot. But not the same way he'd danced with his lady in red. If she would only admit it!

Probing as gently as if he were feeling for a lodged bullet, he said, 'Don't tell me you've forgotten?'

Her eyes flickered. 'Of course not.' But she wouldn't look at him. Or tell him the truth, either.

'And you weren't afraid of me then.'

She sat bolt upright and stopped shunting her knife and fork. 'I'm not afraid of you now!'

'Sure?'

She looked him up and down in a way that he knew she meant to be insulting. It didn't have quite the effect she desired. Rumpling time soon, he promised himself.

'Of course I'm sure. Why would I be scared of a Rambo lookalike?'

He tried to focus on the conversation but it was an effort. When she tilted her chin like that she revealed a length of long white throat which was just begging to be kissed.

He said at random, 'You don't like universal soldier chic?'

'I don't like the military, full stop,' she said with energy. 'If fewer men ran around in uniforms, waving guns about, the world would be a happier place.'

She was trying to make a joke of it. But there was something in that crisp voice that was not amused at all.

Quite suddenly he forget that alluring throat. 'You don't like the military?' he echoed.

'No.' She was mocking. 'Does that upset you? I suppose you think a woman ought to be bowled over by anything in combats? Machismo rules, yeah!'

'That's not quite the way I would have put my case—'

She was saying, 'Guns and explosions and posturing in camouflage gear. It makes me sick.'

And she did indeed look sick.

He stayed watchful but said lightly, 'Don't tell me! You had a schoolgirl crush on a Marine and he dumped you?'

She barely listened. She was shaking. She made a contemptuous gesture. There was no doubt at all that she meant it for his jungle camouflage gear.

'Dress up in that stuff and a man thinks he's got a right to make people jump through hoops if he feels like it. It's insane. And cruel. And—'

She stopped dead suddenly.

Dom leaned back in his chair. Deliberately, he kept his voice idle, his body language calm. 'As

I said. It sounds like you've had an interesting life.'

'I—' She looked horrified.

'Because this is not just a vivid imagination, is it?'

But no matter how calm and idle and low key he kept it, he could not do anything about the turmoil her own words had called up. She stood up. Her eyes had a blind look.

She moistened her lips and did not look at him.

'Got to go. Sorry.'

And before he could get to his feet or say a word to stop her, she was gone.

CHAPTER SEVEN

DOMINIC had been right. It was impossible to find a taxi.

Actually, it turned out be a blessing in disguise. Steaming along the crowded pavements, Izzy found herself calming down.

Why on earth had she let him get to her like that? He didn't matter. He was only set-dressing for Jemima's bungee jump. She wished she'd said that at the time, come to think of it. Why did she only ever think of the really snappy come backs after a twenty-minute delay?

She gave a rather shaky laugh, stopped, and took more measured stock of her situation. It was a lovely golden autumn day. She could walk back to one of the bridges through Battersea Park, if she could only work out in which direction to go. Or she could go home. She didn't recognise the street, but she knew she had to be fifteen, twenty minutes' walk away, tops.

She nearly did. The lure of hot chocolate and her own room was almost overwhelming.

But she had promised Jemima and, like Dominic Templeton-Burke, Izzy kept her promises. She sighed heavily, squared her shoulders and went back to finish her undertaking. Though she did allow herself a brief detour under the green and golden trees.

They had their usual effect. By the time she reached the gate that led out onto Chelsea Bridge Izzy was restored to her normal optimistic state. He had needled her, fine. But she had fought her corner. Needled him right back.

She walked over the Thames and took a bus north, running their conversation over and over in her mind. He had not suspected she was not Jemima. She was sure of that. Well, *nearly* sure. And she had certainly stopped him patronising her. By the time she got back to the hotel Izzy had convinced herself that she had handled Dominic Templeton-Burke rather well.

She tried to call Jemima, to tell her how well she had dealt with Dominic, but the only number she had was the doctor's, and his PA said she could not find either her employer or Jemima.

Oh, well, it didn't matter, Izzy thought. She didn't really *need* to talk about him. And whether she had done well or made a complete dog's breakfast of it made no difference now. She would not be seeing Dominic again. As a reward, she got to go home.

In fact, she was off the hook as of now. All she had to do was check out of the hotel and go back to the flat. And she could go back to being Isabel Dare again. It was such a wonderful thought that she felt her eyes fill with tears.

She began to rush round the suite, flinging open cupboards and drawers. She felt as if she was being let out of prison.

'Goodbye Jemima Mark II,' sang Izzy, to the tune of 'Goodbye Yellow Brick Road', packing enthusiastically.

She divided the things between four suitcases, which were Jemima's contribution to their mutual wardrobe, and an airport carry-on which was her own. It looked as if a lot of Jemima's stuff was only on loan from designers. *Out of the Attic* had taught he to recognise the signs. She hesitated, then rang Jemima's agency.

Certainly Beastly Basil's assistant had no suspicion. Izzy did not even have to say who she was.

'Oh, hi, Jemima,' said the assistant as soon as she heard her voice.

Izzy explained her dilemma.

'Sure, we'll send someone round to pick up the stuff. But don't you want to use any of it over the weekend?'

Izzy looked down at a burnt orange micro skirt and shuddered. 'Don't think so, thank you. I'm— er—going to the country,' she said, inspired.

'I think Basil was expecting you to wait for him there,' said the assistant, taken aback.

Izzy nearly said, *Tough*. She was very tempted. But Jemima would never say 'tough' in a month of Sundays, especially not to Basil. So instead she took a deep breath and cooed, 'Oh, I didn't know he wanted to see me. It's too late to change my plans now.'

'He won't be pleased,' said the assistant warningly. 'You know what he said about not getting too involved with Pepper's business.'

Izzy glared at her image in the mirror. *Beastly* Basil. Just the thought of what he had done to her gentle sister made her fingers curl into claws. If she ever came face to face with the man she might not be able to resist...

But now was not the time to think about revenge, however alluring the prospect. Now she had to broadcast interference.

'I only wish I'd known earlier...' She couldn't manage regretful, but she did quite a good job of sounding nervous.

'Oh, well, can't be helped. Going away with someone nice?'

'Gorgeous,' said Izzy.

A brief picture of Dominic Templeton-Burke flashed up on her inner movie screen. It was followed by an exciting skirmish in which she let herself go on the combat gear and he ended up naked and in her power. She grinned naughtily at the mirror. 'Can't wait to get my hands on him,' she said with feeling, which was all the sweeter because absolutely nobody but her would ever know about it.

'Good for you.' The assistant sounded startled. 'New man in your life, then?'

In her fantasy Dominic was locking the door and turning to her...

'You betcha,' said Izzy, suddenly breathless.

Maybe this had better stop. Fantasies were all very well, but they weren't supposed to take over your head quite so comprehensively. She switched off Dominic Templeton-Burke—reluctantly—and said, 'When is Basil due in?'

'We aren't sure. Maybe Monday. Go off and enjoy yourself. I won't tell him you bunked off,' said the assistant kindly. 'Just don't forget to keep your phone switched on. And don't let lover-boy answer it. You know how Basil gets about boyfriends.'

'Right,' said Izzy, who was beginning to realise exactly how Basil was about every aspect of his models' lives. If he didn't control it, they weren't allowed to do it.

Still, with a bit of luck, by Monday Jemima would be taking her own calls and finding the strength to tell Basil to take a hike. Well, tell him that she was moving to a better agency, anyway.

Izzy arranged a time for the agency's wardrobe to be picked up, then tried to call Jemima again. This time she got through.

Jemima sounded tense.

'Is Basil back?'

'No not yet. Monday, probably. Jay Jay, I'm afraid I had a run-in with a friend of yours. Dominic Templeton-Burke? I think I coped, but—'

'Monday. Oh, God. Have you talked to him? Does he suspect anything?'

Izzy sighed. 'Basil's away. I told you. I talked to the agency. No one there suspects a thing. I'm not quite so sure about Dominic, though—'

'Are you sure? How *can* you be sure?'

'Easy,' said Izzy with total conviction. 'They think you're skiving off with a brilliant new bloke.'

But Jemima was too jumpy to believe her. 'Basil is going to be so mad at me, Izzy!'

It stopped Izzy dead in her tracks. This sounded like serious backtracking. 'It doesn't matter how mad he is,' she said robustly. 'You're getting away from him.'

There was silence.

'Jemima? You still there?'

'Yes.' It was a breathy little whisper.

'And you're getting a new manager. Like next week. Right?'

Another, longer silence.

Izzy forgot all about going home, hot chocolate and even sexy Dominic Templeton-Burke. 'I'll be right over,' she said.

When she got to the clinic there was a message waiting for her. Her sister's consultant wanted to see her. As soon as the receptionist buzzed him, he came to meet her.

'This,' he told Izzy, 'is more complicated than I thought. She seems terrified of this man—her manager. I can't tell how much of that is the state she's in and how much is because the man really is a nasty customer.'

Izzy twisted her hands. 'I don't know either,' she admitted. 'I'd like to scratch his eyes out. But—'

'But you don't know what sort of contract he's tied her up with,' agreed the consultant calmly. 'Look, I've been thinking about this one. I think she needs to see a lawyer. Have you got one?'

Izzy spread her hands helplessly. 'I've never needed one.'

'Well, find one. And not one of the glitzy guys either. A good solid family practitioner whom you can trust,' he advised. 'Get him here, pronto. I'd say we could be looking at an injunction to keep that manager away from her. But nobody can do that until Monday. So can you keep up the pretence in the meantime? Just for the weekend.'

Izzy's heart sank. 'Is it really necessary?'

He hesitated. It was more eloquent than words.

'Do I have to keep it secret from everyone?' She felt as if she were going down without a life belt.

'It would make her feel safe,' he said unanswerably. 'I think it's the only thing that will.'

Izzy gave in. 'Okay. Just the weekend then.'

'Do whatever makes you feel comfortable. Except...' He hesitated, looking faintly awkward.

Izzy sighed. 'Go on—spit it out. What else don't you want me to do?'

He gave her an apologetic smile. 'Don't take over. But don't pressurise her to pull herself together either. She may sound fine when she wakes up. But she's still precarious.'

Izzy nodded glumly. 'I'll be a pussycat, I promise.

So she sat with Jemima until her sister's eyelids fluttered open.

'Hi,' said Izzy softly.

Jemima gave her a foggy smile. 'Izzy. Knew you'd come.'

She was still woozy. Izzy decided that the best thing to do was to chat as normally as possible. So she talked to Jemima about the crazy clothes her stylist liked, the novels she'd read in the last week, the bungee jump.

And then— 'They added on a co-star, too.'

Jemima was sitting up, sipping mineral water. 'What do you mean?'

Izzy watched her carefully. 'We jumped hand in hand. An old friend of yours, I'm told. Hunk called Dominic Templeton-Burke.'

Jemima suddenly looked a lot less woozy. 'Hey-hey! The love interest. Cool.'

Great, thought Izzy. So it was true: lovers! Just as she had feared. She had every right to be very cross with Jemima.

She said crisply, 'It would have been nice to know about him. Couldn't you have brought him to the flat for tea or something?'

Jemima was blind to disapproval. She laughed. 'You sweet old-fashioned thing, you. Do you seriously think Dom is the kind of guy to do tea with the family?'

Izzy glared.

'Get real,' advised Jemima blithely, going off into a little daze. There was a reminiscent half-smile on her face that made Izzy want to slap her.

She sprang up, horrified.

'Well, it was very difficult. I didn't know you—er—knew him. I had to play it by ear.'

Jemima came back to the present with a little jerk. Her mouth tilted naughtily. 'Bet that was fun.'

Izzy breathed hard. Of course it was great to see Jemima back to something like normal, she told herself. On the other hand, the urge to paste her sister to the wall and shake her till her teeth rattled was almost overwhelming.

'It was—not—fun,' she said between her teeth. 'It was a minefield, if you want to know. And I'm not sure that I convinced him that I was you, either.' She stopped in dudgeon. 'What are you laughing at?'

Jemima was grinning broadly. 'Dom too much man for you, huh?'

Izzy stiffened. 'I don't know what you're talking about.'

'Well, face it, Izzy. You like your men a bit tame.'

Izzy was strongly tempted to say that was rich, coming from a woman who fell apart at the thought of sacking an abusive manager. She very nearly did. Only she'd promised the consultant that she would be a pussycat.

So she said with dignity, 'What is wrong with my men?'

'Nothing. They're nice guys. Like poor old Adam, hanging on for you to go on the third date with him. Lets you walk all over him,' said Jemima with a frankness that was, in the circumstances, deeply unfair.

Izzy was taken aback. 'He didn't. I didn't. They don't,' she said, flustered.

'Oh, yes, they do. In the nicest possible way, of course. Only you're always so sure you know best. And most of the time you do. A walking magnet for men who are looking for someone else to make the decisions.'

Izzy blinked. 'And I suppose your men are quite happy to take all their own decisions and yours, too?' she said with irony.

Jemima looked like a cat that had got the cream. 'Yup.'

'No wonder Dominic Templeton-Burke was suspicious,' muttered Izzy.

Jemima chuckled. 'You'll just have to try harder.'

'*What?*' Izzy stared, horrified. 'Oh, no. Not that. No. You can't expect me to do my Jemima Mark II performance for that man again.'

'It's easy,' Jemima assured her. 'Just keep looking at him. Don't interrupt when he's talking. Look impressed.' She did a wide-eyed wondering look that made Izzy feel faintly ill. 'Try it.'

Izzy was outraged. 'Am I a Victorian virgin? Nobody simpers like that!'

Jemima raised her eyebrows. 'No?'

'You're a disgrace.' Izzy was only half joking. 'Whatever happened to equality?'

'Who wants equality? I'd much rather have a lovely macho man madly in love with me.'

'And is Dominic madly in love with you?' asked Izzy, before she could help herself.

Jemima gave a private smile that made Izzy look away suddenly. Maybe that was a question she didn't want answered. 'Never mind,' she said hastily.

But Jemima was clearly in a mood to share. 'All it takes is the right sort of look. Let me show you.'

To Izzy's horrified fascination, she straightened herself against the pillow, tipped her head back and looked at the door lingeringly.

'Stop it,' said Izzy, flustered.

Jemima warmed to her theme. 'It's all in the body language. You look them straight in the eyes. Hold it for a moment, so they know you're looking. Then look down at their feet. Then—slowly—let your eyes go back up to the face.' She demonstrated. 'They should be able to feel you looking.'

'Not much doubt of that,' said Izzy dryly. She was half appalled, half intrigued.

Jemima stopped languishing at the door and gave her sister a brisk smile. 'There you are. If you bump into Dom again you can deal with him.'

Well, at least that didn't sound as if Jemima was in love with the man, thought Izzy. Not permanently, anyway.

Aloud she said, '*No.* I've played all the games with Dominic Templeton-Burke that I can handle.'

But Jemima had one of her lightning mood changes. 'But you've got to. I mean, if you happen to see him again. Izzy—you can't let him know you're not me.'

Two bright spots of colour appeared in her cheeks and her eyes were feverish. 'Basil might find out. He uses the PR agency that Dom's sister works for. They all talk to each other all the time. *Please*, Izzy.'

Izzy was not proof against the real alarm on her sister's perfect features.

'I'll do my best,' she said reluctantly.

Jemima opened her mouth.

'But only until you get this thing sorted once and for all. I,' she told Jemima with feeling, 'have a life, too. And a job. And a pissed-off cousin who won't be pleased if I don't get back to it sharpish.'

Jemima's face turned pinched.

'The weekend,' said Izzy firmly. 'That's how much time I'm willing to spend as Jemima Mark II. And absolutely no interface with Dominic Templeton-Burke. I'll keep the wolves at bay as best I can. But some wolves are just out of my league.'

Jemima gave a watery chuckle. 'What? Even after all my expert guidance?'

Izzy thought of that slow, sultry up and down look that Jemima specialised in. She shuddered.

'*Particularly* after your expert guidance,' she said with feeling. She stood up before she started to volunteer for more than she could handle 'Don't worry. I'll keep well clear of the big bad wolf. And as far as everyone else is concerned I'm the face of Belinda with a head cold.' She hugged Jemima. 'Just look after yourself and get well. I'll be in touch.'

*   *   *

Dom did not know what to do. He did not like it. Dom always knew what to do.

A responsible citizen would go Culp and Christopher—or to the Blane Model Agency—or to Jemima Dare's nearest and dearest, and say, Do you know that your girl is being impersonated by a skilful impostor?

A responsible citizen would not hesitate. A responsible citizen would not think the impostor was so gorgeous that she could not possibly mean any harm.

Lots of gorgeous women meant harm. Get real, Dom.

The real Jemima might have been kidnapped. Okay, the likely explanation was that she was in the Seychelles, or covered in a rash. But she *might* not be. She could be held against her will—anything.

No, the responsible citizen really had no choice. Out the impostor and let her take her punishment! It was the only thing to do.

But—but—

His lady in red did not *feel* like a kidnapper. There was something innately honest about her. Honest and brave and funny and vulnerable and—

And you want to get into her knickers, Dom told himself, half amused, half annoyed. Don't dress it up to be something it isn't. She's a fox.

You want her. Big deal. Doesn't make any difference to the facts. She's lying. The real Jemima Dare has gone missing. And you seem to be the only one who has noticed. You don't have any choice here.

It was tough being a responsible citizen. Well, *fairly* responsible. He thought hard about what to do next and decided that if Culp and Christopher and her model agency hadn't noticed that was their look-out. But her nearest and dearest—that was another thing altogether.

Two hours later he was sitting on Josh's futuristic desk, trying—and failing—to juggle paperclips.

'Jemima Dare's boyfriend out of town?' he asked, concentrating on a nicely weighted green plastic job that seemed to fall more predictably than the rest.

Josh shook his head. 'No regular boyfriend. That's why I got to do escort patrol.' He sounded depressed.

Dom caught the green plastic paperclip neatly, missed the next two, caught the fourth and fifth.

'Ah. So she lives alone.'

'No. Shares a flat with a bunch of girls. One of them is that American tycoon woman. Pepper Calhoun. We may be doing some work on her shop—if we get the bid right.'

'Interesting,' said Dom, bored. But he was much too clever to ask for the address.

He let the man witter, and was rewarded by far more information than Josh had any idea of. Enough to narrow down the address to within three similar mansion blocks, anyway. Well satisfied, Dom went and bought a substantial bouquet and set off south of the river.

The owner of the first doorbell that he rang had no idea where to deliver flowers for Pepper Calhoun. The second response was more helpful. 'End block, top floor, I think. Nice women. The name on the bell will be Dare, though. Not Calhoun.'

He went. It was.

Dom grinned. 'God, I'm good,' he said, for the second time that day.

He rang the bell. There was no answer. Well, he was not surprised. Pepper Calhoun worked, and worked hard by Josh's account. She would be back later. He would come back this evening.

He gave the flowers to a woman in the park.

Keeping the wolves at bay from Jemima was just too damned easy, thought Izzy, trailing wearily up the stairs to the flat at last. It was Friday night and everyone at the model agency was on their way to a party. Not one of them cared what happened to Jemima Jane Dare. Just as long as she was back in harness for the next photo shoot!

Not for the first time, she wondered if her sister's glamorous career was so great after all. At least in the office people noticed if you were *ill*.

She dumped her bag in her bedroom, kicked off her shoes and padded into the kitchen. Pepper was not in yet. Izzy found a bag of tacos and tore it open.

'Oh, the freedom,' she said with a mischievous smile. 'Goodbye, designer food!'

She punched the button on the answering machine. The messages were a predictable bunch: her mother, to say that she and Dad were going away for a few days; Simon, an old boyfriend; Adam, still trying to fix up a date; a girls' reunion from her last job. Then three for Pepper. Ten for Jemima.

'Nothing urgent, thank God.'

Izzy took her bag of cheese and onion tacos out onto the balcony and leaned on the parapet. There was a fine heat haze over the roofs. It was going to be a perfect golden evening. Maybe she should call Adam and get him to take her out of the city, to dinner somewhere discreetly luxurious along the river. And get the dreaded third date out of the way.

She liked him. He wanted her. She was too young to give up men, too old to keep them on tenterhooks for ever. And Adam was a good person.

Except…Except…

Except she didn't want to strip off his jungle gear and make him acknowledge that she was right. Except she couldn't see his face when she closed her eyes. Except her body didn't know him—not as it knew—

Izzy snapped her thoughts off right there. She swallowed.

But she could not get away from it. And she was honest enough to admit it. The truth was that when she kissed Adam they were like two adjacent buildings. They made a bridge but they didn't *fit*.

But when Dominic took her in his arms she seemed to know his contours, to mirror them. They were like two continents that had broken apart, just waiting for time to drift them together. And when they were together they locked into a whole that she knew in her soul.

'Stop it!' Izzy said aloud, shocked.

But— *Think about Dominic,* prompted a little voice inside her head.

Izzy screwed up her face. 'No, no, *no*,' she yelled. Then more calmly, 'That's a complication I can really do without.'

Anyway, he was Nightmare Man. Or at least he wanted to be, with all that jungle camouflage gear and the Tarzan grip.

Yes, that was better. Think of him as one of the company of men she really, really tried to avoid. The macho guys with only one use for women. Like the one who had given her the nightmare in the first place.

In spite of the late summer warmth, Izzy shivered. It was a long time ago and she had dealt with it, she told herself. Dealt with it fine, too. There was no reason to let Dominic's Rambo outfit bring the whole nasty business out from under its stone again.

Only—just every so often—it reached its fingers out of the past and touched her on the back of the neck like a ghost. That was when she froze—and decided that, just for tonight, she didn't want to go out with Adam, or Simon, or any of the other nice men in her life, no matter how much she thought she trusted them. Just for that night all she wanted was to stay at home and not think about anything. And not be touched.

It looked as if tonight was going to be one of those nights. And she was pretty sure why.

Thank you, Dominic!

Well, no matter what Jemima said, Izzy was going to avoid him from now on. Once was more than enough. Those wicked, mischievous grey eyes were just too perceptive.

Izzy was not at all sure that she would survive another encounter with Dominic Templeton-Burke. She was damned certain that her dignity would not. But she was afraid of losing a lot more than her dignity. He was a real risk to all those careful, reliable defences she had constructed over the years. And—just possibly—to her heart.

Izzy went cold at the thought.

Thank you, Dominic—and goodbye!

'Izzy? Izzy are you there?'

It was Pepper. Well, that put an end to all the heart-searching. And a good thing, too, Izzy told herself firmly. She popped another taco into her mouth and wandered out to greet her cousin.

'How did it go?' asked Pepper, unloading brief-cases and bags of samples.

'Too much styling mousse and not enough pri-vacy,' said Izzy. 'But I think I got away with it.'

Maybe her tone was a touch too jaunty. Pepper looked at her searchingly.

'And how is Jemima? Steven said it sounded bad.'

Izzy gave her a quick rundown.

'Nasty,' said Pepper. 'So what are you going
o do over the weekend? You're welcome to come
o Oxford, you know.'

Izzy chuckled. 'Oh, great. Steven would just
love that. We have this English concept of the
gooseberry, you know.'

'Well, anything I can do, just ask.' She col-
oured faintly. 'I mean *we*. Anything we can do.'

Izzy smiled at her affectionately. Against all
the odds, Pepper, the driven high achiever who
didn't waste time dating, had fallen in love with
the master of an Oxford college. It had taken her
time, but eventually she had come to see that he
was in love with her, too. And now, with charming wonder, she was getting used to thinking of
the two of them as a couple.

'You're great. But, no, thanks. I'll heave up the
drawbridge and pretend that Jemima is away—I
don't know where. Nobody's actually going to
come looking for her.'

'Well, if you're sure…'

'I'm sure.' Izzy ran her hand through her hair
and grimaced at the feel. 'I don't know how
Jemima stands all this muck in her hair. To say
nothing of the make-up. I felt as if I was going
around with a plaster cast on my face this morning. What I want is a good long shower to get rid
of it.' Conscience kicked in. Pepper had been

travelling around the whole day, after all. 'Unless you want the bathroom first?'

But Pepper shook her head. 'I want to talk to Steven.' Her eyes were soft.

Izzy did her best not to feel envious. It was great to see her cousin so in love. She did not grudge her the quiet-voiced evening conversations with her beloved. Nor the unthinking intimacy with which she slipped into the shelter of his arm when Steven came to the flat. But it did make her feel—alone.

Alone is what you choose, Izzy reminded herself grimly. Keep on choosing, over and over again. As Simon can attest and Adam will find out. So don't go sighing for something you can't have and clearly don't really want. If some perfect man popped up through a trapdoor and offered to put his arm round you right now, you'd only fight him off. What's more, you know it.

Some people just weren't meant to be part of a couple. Okay, she might want to rip the pants off Dominic Templeton-Burke just at the moment. That didn't mean she wanted to spend every weekend with him. Or call him at the end of a long day just to hear his chocolate-brown voice.

She stamped off to the shower, muttering as

she stripped off. Then she turned the shower on as hard as it would go and a lot colder than her skin was prepared for.

'Ow,' yelled Izzy, forgetting her gentle melancholy in a rush of pure adrenaline.

She emerged, with skin tingling, to hear voices in the corridor. Her heart leaped. Could Jemima have made a break for it from her nice safe clinic?

She knotted the bath towel and rushed out, still swirling her damp hair up in another towel.

'What's wrong?'

She stopped dead.

It was not Jemima. It was a tall, rangy figure whose pants she kept fantasising about removing. Whom she had promised herself she would not see again.

Her hands fell. Followed by the overloaded hand towel and a mop of red hair soaked to blackness. In a move that was pure instinct, she grabbed for the knot between her breasts and clung to her bath towel like a life jacket.

In the circumstances, it really did not need the warning note in Pepper's voice as she said, 'Izzy, this man says he's a friend of Jay Jay's. Dominic Templeton-Burke.'

'Oh, *shoot*,' said Izzy, from the heart.

*   *   *

Bullseye!

Dom could have punched the air. Shouted in triumph. Laughed like a maniac.

And it was all the sweeter for coming out of the blue. Not even in his most extreme scenario of this meeting had he dreamed that *she* would be here. He felt as if he had suddenly been given every missing birthday and Christmas present of his life.

He had really, really not wanted to come and break the news to Jemima's family. He'd practised all sorts of ways of saying it—I'm sure Jemima won't be harmed. No, I don't know where she is, but I'm sure she's safe. Her stand-in felt like the sort of woman you could trust.

He'd even said it aloud. And it hadn't sounded any better than it had in his head. He'd ended up snorting with self-mockery.

Jemima's family would think he was soft in the head. At best. The worst was they would think he was in the plot, too. But—he could not think of anything else to do.

It had occurred to him that they might know Jemima's co-conspirator. Another model from the agency, maybe. Or an old schoolfriend. It had never occurred to him that she would be wrapped in a precarious bath towel with Jemima's cousin covering for her.

Yet here she was. Plain as a bear with a sore head—and twice as angry. No mistaking her. He would know those freckles anywhere.

Also the challenging eyes, that could go dreamy when you least expected it; the creamy skin; the tender mouth that didn't know its own sensuality—yet.

Ah, but it would. If he had anything to say on the matter, that mouth would learn all there was to know about her sensuality...and more...

With an effort, Dom brought his errant thoughts back under control.

'Hi.' He thrust out a hand like a sword: a knight saluting his opponent. 'Nice to meet you. Er—Lizzy?'

'Isabel,' said his tender-mouthed opponent, melting eyes snapping like a piranha. 'Isabel Dare. I'm Jemima's sister.'

Her sister! Well, that explained a lot. Not just the resemblance, either. He searched his memory for what he had been told about Jemima Dare's family and came up with a vague feeling that she and her sister were said to be best friends. So his instinct to trust her with Jemima's safety had to have been right, after all. That was a relief—and not entirely from Jemima's point of view.

He gave her a warm, lazy smile. 'Hi, Izzy. Have we met before?'

She sent a quick look at her cousin. 'No,' she said forcefully.

'Really?' Dom was beginning to enjoy himself. 'Are you sure? I could have sworn…'

She compressed those voluptuous lips until they almost disappeared. 'I'm sure.' There was more than a hint of gritted teeth about it.

He suppressed a grin. Oh, boy, she was beautiful when she was in a temper. Maybe he wouldn't mention it just at the moment, though.

'Well, if you say so. Though I'm usually good with faces.'

'Not this time,' she said curtly. It was very nearly an insult.

The cousin looked startled.

He saw Izzy register it. She pulled herself together with a visible effort.

'Sorry. That sounded rude. Put it down to tiredness and an interrupted shower.' She even managed a smile. It didn't hit her eyes but it showed that she was trying.

'Trying day?' asked Dom innocently.

She snorted. 'You could put it like that,' she said with feeling.

Then caught herself. She narrowed her eyes at him suspiciously. He withstood the hard stare with a smile so bland he was sure she must realise that he knew her secret.

But in the end she gave a sharp sigh and said, 'What can I do for you, Mr Templeton-Burke?'

'Dominic, please. I was expecting to catch up with Jemima. We have a date for this evening.'

'That's a lie—' she said, before she could stop herself. And had to cover it with a lot of coughing.

The cousin looked even more bewildered. Izzy stopped the theatrical coughing and sent him a look of such burning outrage that he nearly laughed aloud.

'I mean—I'm sure you must be mistaken. Jemima would have said.'

'Oh? Maybe you haven't seen her since she put it in the diary,' he suggested dulcetly. 'We only met again this morning.'

Izzy sent him a look like a flame-thrower.

Pepper said hastily, 'Oh, well, there's your reason, Izzy. Neither of us has seen Jemima for a week or more.' She met her cousin's eyes and said firmly, 'Have we, hon?'

So Pepper Calhoun was in on this conspiracy, too, thought Dominic. What was going on? Not that it mattered to him. Jemima was clearly safe with these two looking out for her. As an officer and a gentleman he had fulfilled the demands of chivalry. He could perfectly well say that he would catch her some other time and back out now.

Only—he didn't want to. This was too much fun.

'I suppose not,' muttered Izzy, not very graciously.

He decided to push his luck. 'We're going away for the weekend,' he said outrageously.

She gasped, and her eyes flamed him. He could almost feel her shaking with the need to yell at him that he was lying in his teeth. But as long as she kept up this pretence, she couldn't.

'Oh, really?' she said at last in a strangled voice.

He nodded. 'Yes. We're old—friends.' He let his voice go smoky when he spoke, so it sounded as if a lot more than friendship was involved. He was rather proud of that. He had never thought of himself as an actor before.

'Really?' said Izzy, her teeth snapping shut on the word.

'Yup. Only our careers took us in different directions for a while. We've both been travelling. But when we met again today we realised the old magic was still there. We just had to be together. Couldn't wait a moment longer.'

And he met her eyes with limpid innocence.

'Did you indeed?' said Izzy wrathfully.

He nodded enthusiastically. 'So, is she ready?'

Izzy's gaze sought urgent help from her cousin. 'Er—Jemima's not back—I don't think—'

Pepper said firmly, 'We never know when to expect her. She has a full social diary, you know.' Then, as if struck by sudden inspiration, 'Why don't you leave a message? We'll have her call you the moment she gets in.'

He shook his head. 'That's okay. I can wait.'

And pretended not to see the look of alarm that ran between them.

Impasse, he thought. This had to be the point where they gave in and told him the truth. He was surprised by how much he wanted Izzy to trust him enough to tell him the truth, now he came to think of it.

But he had reckoned without female inventiveness.

'I'm sorry,' Izzy told him with totally spurious regret, 'but I'm afraid you can't. Pepper and I have a business meeting here this evening. A *confidential* business meeting. So I'm afraid we're going to have to ask you to go.'

Pepper barely missed a beat. She looked at her watch. 'In fact, they'll be here any minute.'

It was like a double act. Izzy looked at her cousin's watch. 'Is that the time? They're late, then.'

Pepper began to herd him towards the door, saying over her shoulder. 'And so are you. For heaven's sake go and finish getting ready, Izzy. Goodbye, Dominic. It was real nice to meet you.'

Outgunned and outmanoeuvred. Dominic could hardly believe it!

He had only one shot left in his armoury. 'But you will tell Jemima?' he said anxiously.

'Promise,' said Pepper, driving him inexorably out of the door.

'Tell her I'll pick her up tomorrow morning.'

'Sure—I mean, what?'

Behind her, he saw Izzy's jaw drop. She put out a hand to stop her cousin. But it was too late. Victory snatched from the jaws of defeat, thought Dom, quietly pleased with himself.

'Ten o'clock,' he said, retreating to the top of the stairs. 'Nothing grand, tell her. Just country clothes. And something smart for the dance in the evening. Ten sharp.'

And, waving a cheery hand, he clattered loudly down the stairs without looking back. Though the rolling wave of consternation he left behind him thundered down the stairs after him like a tsunami.

He managed to keep a straight face until he got into the Jeep. And then he sat back in the seat and laughed until the tears ran down his face.

Oh, she was certainly a chess player, his lady in red. But she shouldn't have taken him on. She was going to lose.

And they were both going to enjoy every minute of it.

CHAPTER EIGHT

LEFT alone, Izzy and Pepper stared at each other in total dismay.

'I don't understand,' said Pepper at last. 'How can Jemima have said she'd go away with him? I never heard her mention his name.'

Izzy was shaking with fury. 'You weren't listening, Pepper. He fixed up that date today.'

Pepper's jaw dropped. 'But—'

Izzy nodded. 'But the Dare sister he saw today was me,' she agreed grimly. 'Quite. And I sure as hell didn't promise to go away with him. So he's a liar. And I can't say so without giving myself away. Charming, isn't it?'

Pepper closed the door slowly. 'What are you going to do?

Izzy thrust her hands into her damp mop, frowning horribly. She couldn't think straight. 'I don't—begin to know.'

Pepper was startled. 'You're not seriously thinking of going away with him?'

Izzy flushed. Her heart leaped at the thought. 'Of course not.'

'I mean, you've had a lucky streak so far. But how long before you give yourself away? I mean, if the man is Jemima's—er...' she lowered her voice and managed a very good imitation of Dominic's sexy growl '...*friend?*'

Izzy tried to laugh but it was not a great success. 'He didn't notice the difference this morning,' she said defiantly.

Pepper was unimpressed. 'And has he ever jumped off a crane with Jemima before?'

Izzy bit her lip. 'I suppose not.'

'No. And he hasn't seen her for a few months, he said. It's not going to be so easy when you're sitting side by side in a car for hours at a time.'

Izzy sniffed. 'I can talk like Jemima.'

'For hours?' said Pepper sceptically. 'And what about when you're holding hands under the stars, or whatever the British do when they go away for the weekend?'

Izzy gave an abrupt choke of laughter. 'More likely a twelve-mile hike and then back for tea and a rub down.'

'Right,' said Pepper triumphantly. 'If he's rubbed her down before, you are in deep trouble.' She paused, momentarily sidetracked. 'Do you think he has?'

'I don't know.' Izzy didn't like to think about that for some reason. She nearly said so. Except then Pepper would ask why and Izzy didn't want to think about that either. 'I did ask her. But she wouldn't give me a straight answer.'

'Sounds suspicious.' Pepper sucked her teeth, weighing the balance of probabilities and listing Dominic Templeton-Burke's attributes on her fingers. 'He's cool. He's sexy. He's a hunk.'

Izzy could not deny it. She shrugged, looking away.

'Okay, not Jemima's usual type, maybe,' pursued Pepper. 'But it would be a sin to turn down a man like that, don't you think?'

Izzy bridled. 'Are you saying my sister's promiscuous?'

Pepper looked mildly astonished. 'I'm saying she's human. And he's gorgeous. What's wrong with that?'

Izzy subsided. 'Nothing,' she muttered at last.

'Don't you just love guys who laugh with their eyes like that?'

'Nope. I'm not attracted to compulsive liars.'

Though the very thought of the glint of laughter in Dominic's grey-green eyes was enough to make Izzy go warm.

'That's just as well.'

'What? Why?'

'Well, if you're going to go on pretending you're Jemima, that's the end of any chance of an affair with Dominic.'

'I don't see that,' said Izzy captiously.

'Aha,' crowed Pepper. 'So you do fancy him!'

'No,' said Izzy on a rising note. 'I just don't like being told what I can and can't do. Explain it to me.'

'Because people recognise each other in bed,' said Pepper crisply.

Izzy blinked. Her cousin was no swinger. She pointed this out.

'If he has been to bed with her,' said Pepper, ever the clear-sighted businesswoman, 'he'll know you're not her the moment you kiss him the wrong way. If he hasn't—he'll wonder why she's suddenly changed her mind. Either way, he's going to know the difference. And you're dead in the water.'

Izzy, who had already worked that out for herself, muttered curses on her sister's ill-documented love-life.

'In fact,' said Pepper, 'if I were you I'd get a slow boat to China right now. Because if you stick around you're going to get found out every which way. He doesn't look the kind of guy to give up easily.'

Izzy set her teeth. 'Neither am I. And Jemima's counting on me. I'm not letting Dominic Templeton-Burke get in the way of that.'

'Wow.' Pepper was impressed. She patted her cousin on the shoulder. 'You're a brave woman.'

Izzy marched back to her bedroom with her head high. She didn't feel brave. She felt stupid. And out of control.

Well, she'd been in tighter spots than this, and she was good at keeping a clear head, she told herself. The first thing to do was assess the risk. What she needed to know now—and in detail— was exactly what sort of *friends* Jemima and Dominic had been. No more evasions. No more games. Jemima was going to have to come clean.

She called Jemima's clinic. And walked into a brick wall.

Ms Dare was under sedation. Ms Dare needed to rest. No calls to be put through—doctor's orders.

'But this is an emergency.' Izzy's voice rose in near panic.

The nurse had clearly heard it all before. She was quite kind and utterly immovable. She suggested Izzy call her sister's doctor and explain the nature of the emergency. She even furnished her with a mobile number.

Izzy put the phone down slowly. She thought about it.

Yes, she could call the doctor and explain— 'I'm going away for the weekend with a man who might have been my sister's lover and I need to know what they do in bed.' She shook her head. She couldn't imagine it, somehow.

Okay, what about, I may be falling in love. Only my sister saw him first. I have to know how she feels about him. Did that sound like enough of an emergency? Would that get her through to Jemima?

May be falling in love?

Ouch! Izzy jumped up. Where had that come from? Of course she wasn't falling in love. She hadn't fallen in love with Simon or Adam or all the other nice men she had dated over the last two years. Why on earth would she fall in love with a man who thought she was someone else?

'Sex,' she said aloud. 'Blame it on the salsa.'

She paced her room, really disturbed.

She hesitated at her mirror. 'It will pass,' she assured her reflection worriedly.

Only just for the moment it did not feel as if it would pass. And she could not see a way out. Particularly as long as Jemima stayed incommunicado.

So Izzy was feeling even more out of control next morning. She raided her sister's wardrobe to dress as Jemima Mark II and supply adequate luggage. Then she plonked the suitcases in the hall and sat down on one of them. Her shoulders dropped. She was trying hard to tell herself that she was a successful model but it was an uphill struggle. And her cousin did not help.

'You're crazy,' Pepper told her roundly.

'I know.'

'You do not need to do this thing. Just go downstairs and tell him you didn't agree to a date. He knows it as well as you do.'

Izzy swallowed. 'But then I'll still have it hanging over me.' She did not specify what exactly. Not even to herself.

'You'll get found out.'

'Maybe by then I'll have dazzled him into keeping the secret,' said Izzy, trying for her natural optimism.

Pepper gave her one long, incredulous look and shook her head.

'Well, when it all blows up in your face, you'd better call me. I'll be in Oxford with Steven. But we'll ride to the rescue if we have to. And now I think about it—have you got your running away money?'

It was an old family joke. Pepper was a new relative but she had adopted it with aplomb. For the first time since Dominic had lobbed his hand grenade between them the night before Izzy grinned. 'Yes, Mummy, I've got my running away money.'

'Then good luck and stay safe,' said Pepper, hugging her.

The doorbell rang. They both jumped.

Izzy put a steadying hand to her middle. 'Whoops. Here we go.'

Pepper picked up the intercom release. An imperious voice spoke.

'Yes, Jemima is here. She's on her way down.'

She handed Izzy Jemima's matching cream leather bags. 'You look fine. Remember: think like Cleopatra. Walk like a goddess.'

Izzy took a deep breath. 'I can do this,' she said, as much to herself as to Pepper. 'I *can*.'

Pepper tucked a stray drift of hair back into the complicated plait they had managed between them this morning.

'Sure you can. You're over twenty-one, you're on dry land and you have heated rollers,' she said encouragingly.

'I have indeed,' said Izzy with well-simulated gaiety.

'You're a star,' said Pepper, moved. She knew Izzy well enough by now not to be deceived by the gaiety.

'I'm an idiot with a stubborn streak,' corrected Izzy wryly. 'Oh, well, everyone should do a *Mission Impossible* once in their lives, I guess.'

She put back her shoulders and scampered down the stairs, ready to do battle with Dominic Templeton-Burke. She would give it her best shot. And her best shot was *good*. Especially when it was for the sake of her sister's peace of mind.

Or was it?

Izzy came to a halt so fast the squashy bag over her shoulder swung out and nearly tipped her down the rest of the stairs.

What am I thinking? If it weren't for Jemima, I wouldn't go anywhere near this man without full body armour and flare goggles. He's just altogether too macho.

And a little bit of her said, Then it's going to be interesting to see what happens when you have to leave the body armour behind. Isn't it?

No! Izzy recoiled from the thought so sharply she staggered.

But that treacherous inner voice said, oh yes it will. And you know it.

You may want to forget the night you met, but your body doesn't. No matter what you say, the two of you have a whole lot more in common than an unbridled salsa. The guy only has to look at you and your temperature rises.

With temper, Izzy assured herself, fighting back.

Oh, really? And the way your fingers start to shake, ever so slightly, when he touches you? That's a spontaneous nerve spasm, I suppose?

There was no answer to that. 'Damn,' muttered Izzy between her teeth. 'Damn, damn, damn.'

Think like Cleopatra! Walk like a goddess!

Tremble like a teenager? No way!

She was not going to fall for the man. She was *not*. She went the rest of the way to meet him like the Goddess of Battles.

Dominic was waiting on the doorstep. The battered off-road vehicle sat at the kerb in the smallest possible parking space.

Show-off, thought Izzy, glad to be able to start off hostile. She was a dashing and adventurous driver but her parking was not elegant.

He took the cases from her and did not try to kiss her.

Izzy had been fully prepared to evade any embrace he offered. But the fact that he didn't try annoyed her unreasonably.

He beamed at her. 'Congratulations, you're on time.'

'I'm always on time,' retorted Izzy—and then remembered, too late, that Jemima's poor time-keeping was notorious.

Ouch. First mistake and we aren't even off the doorstep!

But Dominic did not point it out. Maybe he was the one person Jemima had never kept waiting? It wasn't a comfortable thought. What sort of relationship would ditzy Jay Jay have with a man that she cared enough to be on time for? *Oh, Jay Jay, do you really like him?* Just the possibility made Izzy pull a face, as if she were in pain.

Izzy nearly turned round and went back into the house. The only thing that prevented her was Dominic stuffing her cases into the back of his four-wheel drive.

'Gorgeous *and* punctual. You are one unique woman. Nothing new there, then.'

He shut the boot and gave her a lingering smile. It reminded Izzy horribly of Jemima's knowing lecture on body language. Dominic had clearly been to the same life coach.

Izzy set her teeth and smiled back. It made her jaw ache.

Damn, he was looking good this morning. Gone were the combats and the devil-may-care

challenge. Today he was wearing fairly respect-
able jeans and a cotton shirt that someone—
who?—had bothered to iron at some point. The
sleeves were rolled up, though. And the powerful
forearms gave him away.

He might choose to play the English gentleman
for a few hours, if it amused him. But this was a
man who could hack his way through the jungle
with a toothpick if he wanted to, thought Izzy.
Probably had done, come to think of it.

Just as well to remember that, she instructed
herself. If he decided to stop being a gentleman
there was not a lot she would be able to do to
oppose him physically. The idea made her feel
oddly breathless.

Oh, pu-lease, she said to herself in disgust. Get
a grip! The man is not going to throw you over
his shoulder and carry you off like a pirate. And
what's more you'd kick him where it hurts if he
tried.

Er—I hope!

These thoughts were so unsettling that she pretended not to see his offer of a helping hand into
the vehicle. Instead she scrambled up nimbly into
the passenger seat.

'So where are we going?' she asked, all bright
enthusiasm.

His hand fell but he did not move round to the driver's side immediately. Instead he stood there, just looking at her, his eyes quizzical and surprisingly intent.

Intent enough to start up that slight tremor in her betraying hands again. Doing her best to ignore it, Izzy raised her voice and repeated her question.

He seemed to come back to the present with reluctance.

'What? Oh. Gloucestershire. I'm opening a village fête.'

She wished he would stop looking at her mouth.

'How exciting!'

He raised his eyebrows. 'Do you think so? Now, I'd have expected you to be doing that sort of thing all the time.'

Izzy could have kicked herself. 'Oh, well, yes. But that's different.' She sought desperately for a reason why it might be different and came up with rather a good one. 'When I open a fête the punters are not looking at me. They're looking at the clothes.'

Inspired, she thought, pleased with herself.

Two deep clefts drove themselves down either side of Dominic's mouth. It appeared that he was trying hard not to laugh—and it hurt. He leaned into the car and shook his head slowly.

'Nope. Think you're wrong there.' And he gave her another of those long, appreciative looks from the Jemima Dare school of meaningful glances. It did nothing at all for her peace of mind.

But at least it stopped the trembling. Izzy was just so mad at him that for a moment she managed to forget that she fancied him like crazy, too.

'Thank you,' she said frostily. 'Shall we go, then?'

'My pleasure.'

And from the wicked look in his eyes he really meant that. Izzy could have screamed.

But screaming would have meant he'd scored a point. So instead she folded her hands in her lap so hard that her nails dug into her palms.

What would Jemima do now? she asked herself. She certainly wouldn't sit there glaring at the road ahead. She would swing round in her seat, look adoringly at the handsome driver and ask him interested questions about himself.

Well, so will I, thought Izzy grimly. If it kills me.

She had a couple of goes. The adoring look gave her a problem. But in the end she managed some girlish conversation.

'Gloucestershire,' she mused. 'Isn't that a bit tame for a major explorer?'

'Maybe. But there are a lot more punters there than there are in the Southern Ocean.'

'Punters?'

He swung the big vehicle out onto the motorway. 'We've got a bit of a hole in the sponsorship. So opening the fête is all part of drumming up support.'

In spite of herself, Izzy was interested. 'Do you have to do lots of that?'

He was rueful. 'More than I like. But this time I thought I'd got it all sewn up.' His voice hardened. 'Only then we ran into a small local difficulty.'

Izzy looked at him sharply. She saw that he was gripping the wheel as if it were a personal enemy he wanted to throttle. 'Bad?'

His mouth tightened. 'I can handle it.'

A no-go area, she deduced. She wondered why—and was surprised at how much she wanted to know.

Stop it, she told herself. You don't want him confiding in you. You don't want to get any closer to Dominic Templeton-Burke than you absolutely have to.

So instead she said, 'Is it difficult, fundraising?'

He pulled a face, but she saw that his hands unclenched on the steering wheel.

'Not if you have the temperament for it. I admit I'm not good at doing the cabaret.'

She was curious. 'That sounds as if you know other people who are.'

He gave a wry laugh. 'You are so right. Before I've always been one of a team. The other guys have written the books and done the after-dinner speaking. This time the team stays at base camp and I'm the only one out on the ice. So I'm the one the punters want to see.'

'And you don't like it,' deduced Izzy.

He gave a harsh sigh. 'Hell, no. Though God knows why. It was good enough for Shackleton.'

She was startled. 'What?'

'Ernest Shackleton. He raised all the funds for his Antarctic expedition personally. He did anything he had to. People laughed at him but he wasn't proud. He gave magic lantern shows, tours of a museum he set up on his ship—anything to turn an honest penny. Who am I to turn my nose up at a bit of ribbon cutting and judging the bonny baby competition?'

He sounded so wretched about it that Izzy felt an unwelcome stirring of sympathy.

'It sounds as if Shackleton is your hero.'

'Oh, yes. An amazing man.' His voice warmed. '"For speed and efficiency of travel, give me Amundsen. For scientific discovery, give me Scott. But when disaster strikes and all hope is gone, get down on your knees and pray for Shackleton."'

Izzy was impressed. 'That sounds like a quotation.'

'It is. Priestley. Another Antarctic explorer.' He drew a long breath. 'Your peers. That's the praise you want.'

It was a glimpse into the heart of the man, and rather sobering. Izzy stayed quiet, digesting it, until they reached the Cotswold village he said was their destination.

She looked round at a quiet street with a stream running along one side of it, flanked by gingerbread houses. They all had thatched roofs, ancient beams and tubs of geraniums outside.

'Your home village?'

He laughed aloud. 'No, I come from a long line of rugged Yorkshiremen. This weekend we're staying with the Blackthornes. They're distant cousins on my mother's side.

Izzy recalled his instructions on her wardrobe. 'No doubt very grand cousins,' she said dryly. 'I suppose that's why I'm hauling something smart for the evening?'

He chuckled. 'Grand-ish.'

'And what's smart about this evening?'

'Oh, there's a dance. One of the daughters is getting engaged.' He sent her a laughing look. 'They've got the best Cuban band in the country. You'll enjoy that.'

Izzy went very still. She could feel her heart going der-*donk*, der-*donk* so hard that it seemed he must hear it. *Blame it on the salsa,* she thought faintly. Did he remember? Did he *suspect*?

She moistened suddenly dry lips. 'Me? Why?' Even though it was only two words, her voice skidded all over the place.

Dom raised his eyebrows. 'Born dancer,' he said laconically.

Izzy digested that. Her mind was in turmoil. Did he mean that remembered the nightclub and that mad, sexy salsa they had done together? Was he telling her that he knew she wasn't Jemima?

Just for a moment she thought: I can stop pretending. It was like walking up into light from a dark cellar. She turned to him impulsively.

But before she could ask he swung the vehicle off the main road onto a badly surfaced single-track road. It jolted Izzy back to her senses.

No, she couldn't stop pretending. No matter how much she wanted to. Not until Jemima was safe. Not until Jemima had found herself a solicitor and put some distance between herself and that manager she seemed so afraid of. Not, thought Izzy, aching, until Monday at the earliest.

She swallowed and sank back into her seat. She had to keep up the pretence through this weekend. She *had* to. Jemima's sanity might just depend on it.

She said in a small wooden voice, 'Thank you.' And then, because she could not resist it, 'But my sister Izzy is the real dancer in our family. She went all round Latin America and sent back photographs of her bopping at village hops. Izzy is the one who would really love your Cuban band.'

She held her breath.

But he was concentrating on taking the big off-roader down the narrow track between dry stone walls. Izzy was not even sure he had heard her.

Eventually, she let out a long sigh and the tension went out of her. Another danger point passed! He still did not detect the deception they were practising on him, she and Jemima. She told herself she was delighted. A blow for female solidarity! But it felt like a hollow victory, somehow.

In silence, Dominic drove up and up, so that the little village in the valley was far behind. They went along a stony track, through an unkempt meadow full of waving blue and scarlet flowers.

Izzy made herself relax. She looked round—and was startled.

'It's beautiful,' she said on a long note of wonder.

'Country girl at heart?' asked Dominic, looking down at her briefly.

Izzy shook her head. 'Not at all. We were small-town born and bred, my sister and I. And went to the Mediterranean for summer holidays. I don't even remember a camping trip in the country.'

He was taken aback. 'But you've seen a wild flower meadow before?'

'In picture books,' said Izzy, gazing at the vista before her. 'Old picture books. Or maybe a medieval tapestry. Nothing like this. Look at that blue flower. It's like a branch full of stars. What is it?'

But Dominic shrugged. 'I'm no botanist. Try me on rock formations.'

Izzy gave a choke of laughter. 'I was forgetting. You prefer jungles, deserts and ice floes, right?' Just for a moment she took her eyes off the magical meadow to see how he took her teasing.

He did not look at her again, but his mouth curved appreciatively as he kept his eyes on the rutted track ahead.

'That's right,' he agreed. 'Anywhere danger-ous—that's for me. English meadows are just no challenge.'

Izzy snorted in mock outrage. But privately she believed him.

Pretty meadows might be pleasant for a casual weekend. But he was a man who needed to be stretched. Even the steepest slope on this gentle hillside would not stretch him.

Out of nowhere came the thought: And nor would my Jemima. She's as gentle as these sweet meadows. No challenge there either. Wouldn't do for you at all. You need someone who'll stand and fight you when you're wrong, my love.

My love?

Izzy went cold.

Love?

'Stop,' she said distractedly.

Dominic did turn his head at that. 'What?'

'Stop. I want to get out.' Suddenly she could not bear being so close to him and having to pre-tend. 'I need to—breathe.'

At once he brought the vehicle to a halt and killed the engine. He wound the window down and they were engulfed in a murmurous hum. Birds. Insects. Leaves stirring in the faintest of breezes.

Izzy leaned out. All about her was the glory of late summer. In the sky a hawk of some kind was lazily riding the thermal drafts. Butterflies skimmed across clumps of flowers, their wings cream and pale lemon and tortoiseshell in the still air. The air smelled of mown grass.

She was in love with the last man in the world she ought to let herself think about in that way. She wanted to touch him so much it hurt. And she couldn't. Jemima depended on her. *She couldn't.*

She would have given anything to tell Dom what was in her heart at that moment. Maybe she would never have the chance again. Maybe he would never know who she really was. Maybe if he did he would feel so cheated that he would never want to see her again.

The butterflies danced. Izzy's eyes blurred.

'It's perfect,' she said huskily. She drew a shaky breath. 'I want to remember it always.'

He looked at her oddly. 'Remember it? You sound as if you're saying goodbye.'

'Nothing lasts,' said Izzy sadly. She struggled tell him the truth about something, at least. 'Look at it. You can almost touch the sunlight. Taste it, even. There's a poem about how important it is to remember the good stuff. It must have been written on a day like this.'

Dominic snorted. 'There's more to life than poetry,' he said irritably.

Izzy was recalled to her responsibilities. Jemima was not a great reader. 'Of course. I only meant that it was so beautiful I wanted to hang onto it.'

He said abruptly, 'Okay. Want to get out?'

She looked at the mown hillside longingly. 'Can we? I mean, we're blocking the lane.'

He was unconcerned. 'It's not a lane. It's the back drive.' he said indifferently.

Such arrogance!

Izzy was about to point it out. But then he went on, 'If my lady wants to walk, she must walk.'

And she could not think of a single thing to say.

His lady? His *lady*? Oh, my love, if only you knew...

Stop it, Izzy. Everything is a joke to this man. He is teasing you, that's all.

But if he weren't teasing... If he took her hand and told her his secrets and...

It's teasing, Izzy interrupted the fantasy hardily. The only question is whether he's teasing you because you said the glorious field looked like a medieval painting or he can't resist and it's just generalised flirting.

She must not forget that he was a fully quali-
fied graduate of the Jemima Dare School! She
must not let herself fall into the trap of wanting
him to hold her.

I am out of my depth here.

He buffed her cheek gently. 'Don't look so
worried. If anyone wants to pass, they'll sound
their horn.'

Izzy let out a shaken sigh of relief. Thank heavens he had found his own explanation for her anx-
iety. It fitted, even if it was wrong. And it let her
off the hook—this time.

'I didn't think of that,' she said ambiguously.
'Of course.'

'Come on, then.' He swung down onto the
track. 'You want to let your hair down and run
barefoot through the grass? Let's do it.'

This time she let herself take his hand. Even
so, she staggered when her feet touched the uneven ground. Dominic caught her in a strong grip.

'Hey. No need to take off at a sprint. We can
start as gently as you like.'

There was something about the way he said it
that made Izzy narrow her eyes at him in sudden
suspicion.

'You are still talking about a walk in the
meadow, right?'

'I'm talking about whatever you want to talk about,' he said soulfully.

This was definitely seriously advanced flirting. Way beyond that offered by the Jemima Dare School, Izzy told herself wryly. It would be a good idea to be very, very wary.

She strove to remove herself from his still encircling arm. 'Then let's stick with the botanical tour,' she said firmly.

He laughed and let her go.

'Whatever you say.'

She sat astride the pale wall and looked around her, marvelling. They were three quarters of the way up a hill. Below them she could see a little river, rushing and tumbling in a narrow gorge, disappearing here and there under overhanging bushes and an outcrop of willows. They looked like ancient witches, turned to trees by enchantment as they washed their hair. On the other side of the valley, so close it felt as if she could leap across in one bound, there was a patchwork of fields—a blonde swathe of late wheat; a green-gold pasture; a slab of bristly stubble where the birds picked busily among the stalks. The air hummed with life but there was no sound—not even from the rushing river below.

Izzy drew a breath of total content. Well, nearly total content. What did it matter if he didn't know? Her love was new and he was here! Poets had died for less.

'This is wonderful.'

He swung over the wall into the next field with one easy stretch of his long legs. 'Then revel in it.' It was that low voice that she remembered so well from the nightclub—smooth as velvet, rich as chocolate, melting.

Izzy swallowed. She ached to surrender to that seductive voice. Her pulses raced and her heart yearned. And she had to stand still and pretend she was indifferent. The pain was exquisite.

Dom held out an imperious hand. But his eyes weren't imperious. They were searching.

The temptation to take his hand was almost overwhelming. But it was a step too far into dangerous territory. Izzy held back, evading his glance.

'We can't just go tramping over someone else's field,' she protested.

And I certainly don't intend to let you hold my hand. Or look into my eyes and make double-edged remarks.

Dominic laughed. 'You're a real little rule-keeper, aren't you?'

She gave a crack of startled laughter. 'You are so wrong. I do whatever I have to.'

She could not help herself. The Andean village and the men in their ragged combat gear flashed into her mind. But for the first time in ages she thought about them without flinching.

She found Dominic was studying her closely.

'Another memory? Not a nice one, I'd say.'

She jumped. Her immediate instinct was to turn away, hide the old feelings. But then she paused.

She had not flinched when she thought of them. She had come a long way. Could she complete the journey? Could she haul the festering splinter out into the light of day, once and for all. Could she tell Dominic Templeton-Burke?

He folded his muscular arms over his chest, waiting.

Izzy said, with difficulty, 'I once had to—well, I thought I had to—I made up my mind to—'

But, no, she couldn't do it.

Dom thought she was Jemima. He had to go on thinking it. He had brought *Jemima* here as part of some sophisticated ritual dance of sexual attraction and power play. It was a game to him. Izzy knew she could not afford to strip her soul bare for a man who was playing games.

She turned away. 'Are you sure the car won't be in someone's way?'

'If it is, they can sound their horn,' he said. Was it her imagination or did he sound disappointed? 'You do worry about little things, don't you? I just bet you were a prefect at school.'

That was better. She could deal with this sort of teasing, easy-peasy. It was when his voice went to dark chocolate and he called her his lady that she nearly buckled—forgot her sister, forgot everything.

She stuck her nose in the air. 'If you're calling me teacher's pet, you're quite wrong,' said Izzy with dignity. She did not budge from the wall. 'I'll have you know I was banned from the zoology lab for putting electric currents through dead things.'

'I'm impressed,' he said lightly. 'You must tell me about it some time. Now, are you going to come here to me? Or are you going to sit on the fence for ever?'

Izzy was so startled that she forgot it was dangerous to look at him. This time she was not quick enough to avoid eye contact. His eyes held hers deliberately.

'You can sit there kicking your heels as long as you like.' His voice was level, dispassionate. And she was absolutely certain he wasn't talking about the Cotswold wall. 'But eventually you have to make up your mind. Forward. Or back. Only two ways to go.'

Their eyes locked. She felt the hair rise on the back of her neck. *He knows!* she thought with sudden certainty. *He knows I'm not Jemima. He has to. He can't make me feel like this if he doesn't know.*

'Well?' said Dominic softly.

She nearly challenged him with it then. So nearly.

But she was shaken and vulnerable and he was—implacable, somehow. Think of Jemima, she told herself frantically. This is a spur of the moment thing. If you give in, you'll regret it later. Jemima needs you. Dominic Templeton-Burke doesn't.

Ah, but what do *I* need?

Later, Izzy told herself, almost weeping. *Later.*

She levered herself briskly off the wall and went to him, her chin in the air.

'Okay. You must know more about this place than I do. I'll trust you to know what you're doing.'

'Gee, thanks.' He didn't sound pleased. 'You're a real flatterer, you know that?'

'Just telling the truth.'

Keep it light, she thought. Keep it light. Walk beside him so he can't look into your eyes. Keep your distance so he can't touch you. And you might just get to that dance unscathed.

Dominic strode out without speaking for a few minutes. He was frowning at the ground as if it was obstructing him. Then he said abruptly, 'Why won't you trust me? I mean really trust me?'

'I don't know what you mean,' Izzy said in a strangled voice.

Dom dismissed that with an impatient hand 'Yes, you do. You weigh everything you say to me. You won't look at me. You try hard to make me think you're so at ease—but the moment my shoulder touches yours you leap a mile in the air.'

Izzy gasped with genuine indignation. 'I don't!'

'You should be where I'm standing,' he said dryly. 'Feels like a mile to me.' He turned and looked down at her. The frown had gone but he was grave. Graver than she had ever seen him. He did not try to touch her. 'Why?'

Izzy thought fast.

'You're a man who likes to break rules, right?'

His brows knitted. 'Bend them sometimes, maybe. Who doesn't?'

Jemima didn't. And Izzy had always laughed at her for it. But now, when it was so important, when *Dom* was so important— 'I'm not sure I do,' she said slowly.

He was puzzled. 'So?'

'So from the moment we went bungee jumping yesterday you've been needling me. Pushing me. Wanting me to…' she hesitated.

'Break the rules?' he said softly.

'I— Yes.'

'And which rules would they be?' he said in an idle voice.

My rules.

But of course she couldn't say that. Because then he would ask about her rules and she would be torn between Jemima, who needed her, and this laughing, teasing renegade who didn't need anyone. Except that he wasn't laughing at the moment. He looked deadly serious. Even vulnerable. Izzy realised it with a shock.

It was on the tip of her tongue to tell him the truth then. But she thought where it would take her. She would not just be betraying Jemima. She would be opening the door for him to all her secrets. And she would have to take herself back to that Andean hillside and the reasons why she was not, and could never now be, like her innocent-hearted sister.

Izzy stared at him until her eyes ached. And could not think of a thing to say.

Dom put out a hand, very carefully, as if she were a nervous animal, and just touched a frond of her hair.

'All right,' he said quietly. 'We'll play it your way. I'm a patient man.'

Izzy's throat hurt. He sounded so—*caring*. The temptation to fling herself into his arms and tell him her every last secret was almost overwhelming.

Almost! *Remember Jemima. This is for Jemima. Jemima is counting on you.*

'I can wait. But one day you *will* tell me.'

'I—' She moistened her lips.

Instantly his eyes flared, as if she had waved a match in front of them.

He groaned. 'Just as well I'm into endurance sports. Oh, well, come along, you tantalising woman. There's work to be done.'

CHAPTER NINE

AND work started the moment they came in sight of the house. Izzy was grateful for it. It stopped her thinking about the temptations of the truth. And the risks.

'Oh, wow,' she said brightly. 'Just as I thought. 'A full-on stately home. Palladian façade! Three massive wings! Statues on the terrace! It looks like a film set.'

Dominic was amused. 'And this is just the back yard,' he said solemnly. 'You should see the statues in the front.'

Izzy groaned. 'You said smart. Not imperial.'

He chuckled. 'Wait until you get indoors. You'll be knocked over by an Irish wolfhound who thinks he's a poodle and licked to death by a cat who thinks she's a dog. Formal it isn't.'

And then the back drive curved a little and she saw the field of booths and tents stretching away to their left, down to the little river.

'Oh, look, the house is under siege,' she said chattily.

Dominic was unmoved. 'That's the fête. In fact, I'd better just stop off and unload. I can find out when I'm needed, too.'

He coasted onto flat ground in the shade of an oak tree and touched the horn.

Several people were milling around among half-assembled trestle tables. They all looked up at the sound of the horn and one of them came over. She was tall and white haired, with humorous grey eyes very like Dominic's.

'Hello, toad. Brought your begging bowl?' she greeted him.

'Hello, Aunt Margaret. I've brought you a bonus. This is—'

Did he hesitate fractionally? Izzy wasn't sure.

'Jemima Dare. She's a much more glamorous celebrity than I am.'

The woman addressed as Aunt Margaret raised her eyebrows, also very like Dominic.

'That's not hard.' But she nodded pleasantly. 'Nice to see you, Jemima. You'll have to bunk up with Dom. The house is packed to the rafters. Still, you're probably used to it.'

Izzy gulped. 'H-hello.'

Dom chuckled. 'My sort-of-aunt, the Duchess of Bonaccord. She's a professional bully and organiser of fêtes.'

'Somebody has to,' said his aunt, unmoved. 'We've given you booth number four. You can put all your posters and stuff up there. The children have made *I put Dominic on Ice* stickers. They're going to dress up as Eskimos and go round selling them.'

Dom looked appalled. 'There aren't any Eskimos in Antarctica.'

'Details, details,' said his sort-of-aunt airily. 'Anyway, Flissy *may* turn up as a penguin. They were arguing about it at breakfast.'

'Oh, that's all right, then,' said Dom, relieved. 'There are plenty of penguins.'

Izzy choked. He smacked her knee lightly, out of sight of the Duchess.

'Okay, Aunt Margaret. We'll unload my stuff now. Then go up to the house and unpack.'

'And then you can come back and help put up the stalls,' said the Duchess firmly. 'We need all the help we can get if you're going to cut that ribbon at three!'

They did as they were told.

The house was, as Dom promised, nothing like as intimidating as it looked from the outside. They went in through a side door straight into an enormous kitchen. Enormous but, as it seemed to Izzy, full to bursting.

In addition to the psychologically disturbed wolfhound there were people of all ages in various stages of undress, a more or less cafeteria breakfast service and three children in pyjamas wearing diving flippers.

'Why?' asked Dom, interested.

'Penguin feet,' explained a seven year old seriously. 'We made the beaks last night.'

'That sounds encouraging,' he said to Izzy, as serious as his small relative. 'The fewer Eskimos the better. That sort of mistake is *not* good for my public image.'

'And your public image is all you care about, of course,' teased Izzy, her eyes full of affectionate amusement.

'Too right. It's money in the bank to a man on the fundraising trail.' He looked round the kitchen. 'Definitely too many people. We've got to do some serious staking out of territory here. Come along.'

He hefted his overnight bag onto his shoulder and led her through a dizzying length of corridors and up some back stairs to the attic. He pushed open a door and said, 'Ah. Good.'

Izzy peered over his shoulder and saw a functional bathroom with a welcoming array of rubber ducks and swimming frogs.

'A bathroom?' she said puzzled. 'You want a bath?'

'No, but I will,' said Dom briskly. 'And so will you. I just wanted to check they hadn't moved it since the last time I stayed.'

Izzy shook her head, bewildered. 'I suppose you know what you're talking about?'

His eyes danced. 'First law of surviving the English country house weekend. Seek out the children's bathroom and stake your claim.' He plonked a battered sponge bag down on an equally battered bathroom stool.

Izzy laughed. 'You can't resist the rubber ducks?'

'I can't resist the hot water,' corrected Dom. 'The hot water cylinder is usually in the children's bathroom. The further you get away from it, the further it has to travel, the more tepid it becomes. Aunt Margaret will suggest you use her bathroom. Fight her off with pikes and sabres. It's got cushions and wall-to-wall Dior bath oils. The bath is the size of a boat. By the time it's full, it's cold.'

Izzy choked. 'Thanks for the tip.'

'Least I could do. I don't want you freezing. Even in such a warm September this is a cold house. And I hate cold feet in bed.'

All desire to laugh left her. 'About that...'

'There's no spare room. We have to share a bed. Believe me, it's a whole lot better than sharing a damp tent in the jungle. You'll survive,' he said breezily.

Izzy snorted. 'Of course I will. It's not that.'

He cocked an intelligent eyebrow. 'No horizontal tango? Fair enough. I'll keep my hands off you if you promise to do the same.'

Not for the first time Izzy would have liked to hit him.

'I'm willing to sign the pledge,' she said, with more bite than she'd meant.

Dom stuck out a hand. 'You've got yourself a deal.'

He shook her hand firmly. And then didn't touch her for the rest of the hectic day.

Izzy did not know if she was reassured or irritated. By mid-afternoon, though, she was sure as hell frustrated.

He was a charmer. No question of that. He gave a delightfully witty speech to open the fête and cut the ribbon. And then he sat patiently in his booth, surrounded by glossy posters of himself and his companions in various dangerous exploits. He signed autographs, taking the time to have a real conversation with everyone. It slowed down the queue like nobody's business. But Dominic wouldn't be hurried. If a ten-year-old wanted to know how you went to the lavatory on pack ice, then Dom was more than willing to explain.

Izzy watched a liberal parent's eyes cross and hastily held out a copy of a poster.

'Eighty per cent of the price goes to fund the expedition,' she said encouragingly.

It deflected Dom and his interlocutor. A poster, a couple of books and an *I put Dominic on Ice* sticker changed hands.

'Thank you,' gasped the parent with real gratitude, and staggered out in the direction of scones and tea.

Dom grinned at her. 'What a team we make. They pay me for the stories and then they pay you to get away from them! Want to join the campaign bus?'

Izzy smiled. But inwardly she flinched. If the invitation were to Izzy and not Jemima it would be heaven, she thought. But he barely knew Izzy existed and there was a queue to deal with.

So she waved at him to talk to the next eager enquirer. Meanwhile she tidied the pile of books he had brought for sale. There was a wide variety—about the Antarctic, about his previous expeditions, about extreme conditions and survival techniques.

'And not one of them written by you!' said Izzy in congratulatory tones. 'So you have some feelings of modesty after all.'

Dom's grin died. 'My companions tell it better—including what a bastard I am to travel with,' he said lightly. But his eyes were bleak.

What have I said? thought Izzy, alarmed. I never meant to hurt his feelings! I was only teasing. Oh, why do I keep getting everything so wrong? I'm not normally so clumsy. Pretending really, really doesn't suit me.

Still, if she *had* hurt his feelings Dominic did not let it show. He was endlessly patient with the fairgoers. He answered every question, no matter how daft, with courtesy and precision. He was nice to everybody.

Izzy sat there with him, collecting contributions, bagging up purchases and making a list of the addresses of subscribers. He was nice to her, too. Only he never once met her eyes or touched her, even by accident. And yet she was aware of him with every breath she took.

We've come a long way since the nightclub, she thought. Heck, we've come a long way since the bungee jump.

She remembered her first recoil when she saw him in combat gear. How could she have been so stupid? As if clothes said anything about the man underneath!

Had he seen the way she flinched? Sensed her retreat? For the first time it occurred to her that he might have seen it as a challenge. Maybe that was why he had been so determined to pursue her. Or pursue Jemima, Izzy reminded herself, depressed.

Her reaction had been pure instinct—he had looked like her nightmare—but it was not a reaction he would have been used to. Maybe he'd taken it personally. And that was why she was here now.

She looked at him. No, the man certainly did not look as if he had ever been a woman's nightmare before. On the contrary, he had the ease, the charm, the sheer animal magnetism of a man that women walked barefoot over the faces of their friends to get at. And several women at the fête were showing signs of doing just that. The man was a chick magnet.

Oh, yes, a long, long way since the nightclub and the bungee jump.

That was when she thought— *This is our third date!*

The third date. The sex date. The date she had started to run away from. Only this time she didn't want to run. She wanted to...

Izzy began to feel slightly light-headed.

'Why don't you write a proper book, just about you?' said one breathy blonde, pouting her bosom at him.

He gave her a smile that Izzy, too, would have put in a good deal of barefoot mileage for.

'Not my scene. I'm the muscle, not the brains.'

Izzy sat bolt upright, as if she had touched live electricity.

She had heard that tone of voice before. She heard it in herself when she said, 'I've never been the pretty one.' It said—This is true and I wish it wasn't. I wish I didn't care, either, but I do. So I'm trying hard to pretend I don't.

When the voluptuous blonde left, Izzy said idly, craftily, 'Yes, why not a book of your own? You must have had plenty of offers.'

That made Dom look at her at last. It was not a particularly friendly look.

'Why do you care?'

She knew that tone, too. She used it herself. It said, Don't Corner Me. It said, Keep Out!

So she shrugged. 'I don't. Just intrigued. That's all. Surely a book deal would solve the funding problem? Then you wouldn't have to send posses of under-age water fowl to mug the residents of Gloucestershire.'

There was a pause. Then he laughed. But it was reluctant.

'I ask myself why,' said Izzy in her best indifferent tone.

She stuffed her hands in her pockets and propped herself up against the side of the booth. On the rough stage, some terrifyingly well-drilled little girls were dancing over swords, kilts swirling, chins rigid.

Dom said nothing. Izzy held herself quiet, though her every sense was alert.

And then, very quietly, he said, 'I can't.'

'What?'

He said baldly, 'I can't write.'

She was so astonished she forgot that she mustn't corner him. She whipped round.

'Can't *write*?'

His mouth twisted. 'Not properly. I can do the basic stuff if I put my mind to it and don't rush. Well, you've just seen me. I can sign autographs.' He paused. Then added with an effort, 'Now.'

So that explained the glacial pace of the queue! And the long, friendly conversations as he traced out his name!

Izzy sat down rather hard. The camp stool rocked.

At once, a strong arm shot out and he brought it to rest, steady as a rock. He let it go. His smile twisted.

'I'm dyslexic,' he said baldly. 'A really bad case, apparently.'

'I—'

'Oh, I can do lots of other things. My reflexes are white-hot and I play a mean game of chess. Apparently I'm what's called an "action-oriented extrovert". No thinking involved. Just plenty of *Boys' Own* adventures.'

The bitterness was searing.

Izzy said, 'How long—?'

'Have I known?' He shook his head. 'Not long enough. School just wrote me off as stupid, and the family thought I was a hell-raiser who refused to work.'

'Your mother didn't realise?'

'My mother was ill most of my childhood. And then she died.'

Izzy wanted to hold him. She knew it would be fatal. She sat on her hands.

'So when did you find out?' she asked in a friendly, neutral voice.

Dom pushed aside the desk of souvenir stickers and other people's books and stood up. He did not look at her. But at least he didn't sound bleak and bitter any more.

'That was really weird. I have this friend—he's an Arab sheikh. Really dashing, but a scholar, too. A sort of Gulf Leonardo da Vinci. Well, he and I did an expedition on horseback across the Gobi, and one night he was showing me some Arabic script. I realised that I found it no more difficult than I found ordinary letters. I could make out the words with about the same amount of effort. And he said—''That's very unusual. You need to get that tested.'' So when I came back, I did.'

'And?'

'And there are therapies. I've done them. I still do, when I have time. So these days I can sign my name and fill out a tax return. Even write the odd note, if I have to.' He paused. 'But there's no point asking me to woo you with poetry. That's way, way out of my league.'

Izzy was thinking. 'Can you dictate?'

Dom was startled into laughing. 'Dictate a sonnet? I shouldn't think so.'

Izzy was impatient. 'No, I mean a book. A diary of the South Pole, or whatever. Couldn't you dictate it?'

'You don't give a publisher three months of tapes,' he pointed out.

She subsided. 'No, I suppose not. Damn!'

'But thank you for your concern,' he said gently.

She half turned, thinking, He's got to touch me now.

But a stout child wrapped in a black legal gown that was six sizes too big for it and wearing an aggressive beak and flippers was bearing down on them. And the moment passed.

It was like that for the rest of the afternoon. Even when they went back to the house to get ready for the evening dance, even when he was helping her pack her stuff for the expedition to the children's bathroom, Dominic did not touch her.

Would he come to her there? Make love to her among the rubber ducks and the friendly battered furniture? Izzy hoped he would. She even hesitated about locking the door. But in her heart of hearts she knew he wouldn't come. She turned the key with a sense of loss that she could hardly believe.

When she went back to their shared room he was already in his formal black trousers and pristine white shirt. He talked as easily as if they had known each other for ever while she fluffed up her hair, trying to make it look like Jemima's, and applied careful make-up. He was friendly, funny and sexy as hell. And a No Entry zone. He could not have made it clearer if he'd pinned a notice on a sign above his head. He did not even ask her to fix his bow tie. He did not ask her anything.

So it was a subdued Izzy who went downstairs with him for the engagement party.

It was, as Dom had said, very grand. The Duchess was wearing a magenta crinoline and some truly amazing rubies. At least three of the younger women were in the sort of gowns that Izzy had come to recognise as serious designer labels. Jemima's slinky number from Delys held its own—but only just. And of course Izzy's borrowed jewellery was all fun costume stuff.

She hesitated, standing beside Dom at the top of the stairs, looking at the froth of diamonds and silks below.

'I'm not up to this.'

He said with sudden harshness, 'You can do whatever you have to. Remember?'

She was startled. 'I said that?'

'To me. This afternoon.' He sent her an odd look. 'I'm still waiting for the explanation.'

She shivered. 'Maybe one day.'

He nodded gravely, as if he'd expected nothing else.

'Not too long. Like I said, I'm a patient man. But even my patience has its limits.'

It wasn't a threat. But there was something in his eyes that said he meant it. Izzy's heart lurched.

'You're very determined, aren't you?' she said slowly.

Dom stared at her in amazement. 'Of course I am. It's part of the job description.'

And they both laughed.

It eased the tension enough for her to look round and say teasingly, 'And where does all this fit in to the job description?'

'This?'

She waved a hand around the seething hallway. 'Family. Engagement parties. White wedding on the lawn. Children dressed as penguins.'

He steered her towards the terrace, where there was champagne and laughter.

'You're asking me how I've managed to avoid the marriage trap,' he interpreted. There was just a touch of smugness in his tone.

Izzy shook her shoulders with irritation. 'Why would anyone want to trap you?' she said frostily.

'Because I'm clean, good company and handy about the house,' he said promptly.

Izzy choked down a laugh. 'But too determined to fall into the trap,' she said, shaking her head with mock sadness. 'What a loss!'

He gave her a blinding smile. 'No, you're wrong there. Just determined enough to hold out for the best.'

Izzy thought she had not heard right. *'What?'*

'You,' he said with mock disapproval, 'have a stereotypical view of the explorer.'

'I don't have a stereotypical view of anyone,' objected Izzy.

'Oh, yes, you do. You think we're wild men who love 'em and leave 'em and spend our time in full flight from commitment.'

She folded her arms across Jemima's turquoise silk plunge neckline like a baker's wife squaring up for an argument. 'Oh, that's right,' she said sardonically. 'Whereas you're a fully paid up sensitive soul, just waiting for Miss Right!'

'Maybe not waiting much longer,' he murmured wickedly.

She refused to hear that, though she could feel the blush beginning. I bet it's turning my ears red, she thought. If he points it out, I'll deck him.

'In fact,' he said, manoeuvring her cleverly so that she had her back to the column of the terrace and could look nowhere but at him, 'I'm glad you brought the subject up.'

Not just her ears, her whole face and neck must be incandescent.

'I didn't,' howled Izzy. 'What subject? Oh, you can be so *irritating*.'

'I have strong opinions on marriage.'

'I just bet you have,' she muttered.

'Let me tell you about explorers and marriage.'

She stared, 'What?'

'Matthew Flinders. He was the man who mapped the coast of Australia.'

She knew that note in his voice. Suddenly she forgave him his mock vanity and his teasing. 'Another of your heroes?' she said, with tender amusement.

He laughed back at her. 'Got it in one. He married his childhood sweetheart. The bureaucrats wouldn't let him take her with him so he wrote to his Anne every day. He told her to tell him what she wore, what she dreamed—anything as long as she talked to him about herself. And when he went home ten years later she was still waiting.' He said softly, not laughing at all, 'That's what I want.'

Izzy was uneasy. 'You don't want much,' she said in a teasing voice.

But for once it fell flat. Dom was deadly serious, she saw.

'When I was eighteen there was a girl I wanted to marry. Only I went off to the Indonesian jungle and she made a determined play for my elder brother.'

Izzy could have wept for him. But she knew sympathy would be a killer. She said in a judicial voice, 'You don't seem to be great judges of women in your family.'

That startled him. Dominic gave a great crack of laughter. 'You are so right. You should see the harridan who is my father's second wife. In fact she's the reason the expedition is in this funding muddle in the first place. She talked my father into pulling his company's contribution.'

He sounded almost light hearted about it. Izzy could not understand such insouciance.

'Aren't you furious?'

'A certain amount of aggro went down at the time,' he acknowledged. 'But it's had its compensations. If it hadn't been for that, I wouldn't have met you.'

His eyes were warm. Warmer than they had been all evening. Had the No Entry zone notice come down, then?

Hardly daring to ask herself, much less Dom, Izzy said, 'I don't understand.'

'The wonders of PR,' he pointed out. 'Totally loopy, but the side benefits are interesting.'

'I am not,' announced Izzy wrathfully, 'a side benefit.'

That was when he touched her. It was a bear hug of a touch. It lifted her off the floor and nearly cracked her spine and she wanted it to go on for ever.

'You certainly aren't,' he said. 'Definitely the main attraction from now on.'

He did not leave hold of her for the rest of the evening. They ate holding hands. They toasted each other, looking into each other's eyes as if they were the only people in the room. They danced. Wild and wanton or close and dreamy, it made no difference. They belonged. And everyone in the great panelled ballroom knew it.

'Bed,' he said at last. He did not even bother to lower his voice.

And Izzy, smiling, said, 'I thought you'd never ask.'

CHAPTER TEN

SHE'LL tell me now, thought Dom. She won't keep lying to me when we make love. She couldn't. She'll remember the first time when we danced, when we kissed. And she'll tell me the truth.

Outside the bedroom door he turned her into his arms and began to kiss her. Not her mouth, but her eyelids, her nose, her shoulder; the tremulous, treacherous pulse in her throat; her ears, which went such an enchanting pink when he teased her. The tender valley between her breasts.

She gave a sharp intake of breath, as if he had shocked her. Though that couldn't be true. No modern woman would be shocked by a simple kiss.

Except that it wasn't a *simple* kiss. And it set them both trembling like birch trees in a high wind.

'A new experience,' he said, his words muffled against her skin.

'What?'

But he did not answer. Or not in words. Instead, his arm tightened round her body like a vice. Not taking his mouth from hers, he turned the doorknob behind her back and walked her backwards into the room.

She was already hauling his dinner jacket down his arms, panting slightly.

He kicked the door shut and ran his hands the length of his body, holding her against him, breathing in the scents of her.

She made a husky sound and ripped open his shirt.

All the little things went wrong, just as they always did the first time. It didn't seem to matter.

They fell onto the bed in a tangle of desire and wrenched clothes. He heard her shoes hit the floor. She lost interest in the shirt and began to trace the shadowed musculature of his torso, crooning as he stroked the sweet curve of her shoulder, the soft and vulnerable nape under the silky hair, her swelling breast...

Then he heard her give a little exclamation of pain.

'What is it?' he demanded, shocked out of his hot, fierce world of need for a moment.

A strand of silky hair was caught in his watch.

He gave a laugh that was half a groan of desire. 'Stay still for a moment.'

But she didn't want to wait while he unwound it. She wanted to writhe herself around him, tease

him as he was teasing her. In the end she broke
the thread impatiently and went back to rubbing
her cheek against his hair roughened chest.

Dom drew a gasping breath. His head fell back.
'Careful…'

But she was not the careful type, his lady in
red, and she did not want him wearing anything.
His shirt hit the opposite wall in a crumpled bun-
dle. She applied herself to the expensively discreet fastening at the waist of his dress trousers
without much success.

'What is wrong with simple poppers?' she muttered direfully. 'Give me jeans any day. How do
these things *work*?'

He gave a shaken laugh. 'I'll give you a crash
course,' he promised. 'Let me.'

But in helping her he got sidetracked.
Inevitable, really. For all her obligingly abandoned neckline, she was wearing too many
clothes. He tried to release her from the turquoise
draperies and found that she was encased in underpinnings that were quite beyond him.

'This would challenge a court armourer,' he
said, trying to concentrate. Not very successfully.
She was making voluptuous kissing noises which
made his blood thrum in his ears. 'How does it
work?'

She wriggled herself onto her back and flung her arms up among the pillows.

'No idea.'

He sat up, laughing. 'Okay. Do it yourself.'

She tipped her chin at him. Her eyes were warm with wicked laughter and the wonderful hair spread wide.

'Can't you handle it?' she taunted mischievously.

But behind the laughter there was a profound question.

Dom recognised it. He bent over her, a hand on ether side of her head, and looked deep into her eyes.

'As long as you want me to, I can handle anything,' he said with soft gravity.

For a moment she stared at him, as if she could not believe what he was saying. Could not believe that they were here, in this bed, together.

Then she made a strange sound, almost like a sob, and grappled him down to her. Her hands were convulsive, her breath fast.

'Love me,' she demanded in a voiceless whisper. Her eyes were wide, staring. 'Love me *now*.'

Hang on, thought Dom. This is wrong. She shouldn't look like that. She should have told me the truth by now...

But she had got rid of the underpinnings some-how, and the way she was curling and writhing to get out of the silky skirts was more than flesh and blood could take unmoved.

I'll think about it later, he promised himself, bending to take one lifting nipple in his mouth. And, as she moaned, *A long time later.*

And after that nothing was little any more. And nothing went wrong.

She fell asleep abruptly, still sweat slicked, her body utterly surrendering to profound peace, as if she had not slept well in a long time. For a while Dom leaned on his elbow, watching her. In spite of his sated body, he was aware of faint regret. He wished she had told him her name.

Well, he knew it, of course. *Izzy.* They had been introduced, for heaven's sake. And she had told him again this afternoon, only it was Cuban dance music that had got it out of her, not love of Dominic Templeton-Burke. He tried to be amused. She was not a very good liar, his lady in red.

He pushed curling tendrils of red hair gently back from her forehead. Not a very good liar at all. When she made love she gave up her whole heart with her limber body. No evasions, no pre-tences, no make-believe. Just—

Love?

It was a sobering thought. But it was right. He knew it. Dom bent and feathered a kiss across the air above her parted lips.

Her nose wrinkled and she puffed a little in her sleep. He grinned, settling himself down to sleep beside her at last.

It definitely paid off, he thought drowsily, holding out for the best. Most sensible thing he'd ever done. Tomorrow he would tell her. In fact tomorrow he would point out that they were destined for each other and she had better get used to it. Oh, and tell her that he knew her name.

That should be good for a couple of hours' fireworks, he thought, grinning. And fell into the sleep of total satisfaction.

Izzy did not know what time it was when she came awake. The sky beyond the strange window was grey, just lifting into morning. She slid out of bed and padded across the uneven boards. The moon was still out, pale as water, and you could make out one or two of the brighter stars. But it was nearly morning.

She wrapped her arms round herself. She was naked. Inside and out, she thought, trying to make a joke of it. She felt cold to her bones.

Beside her, the man she loved and had lied to comprehensively stirred. He muttered something. She was not sure what. Maybe 'Honey'.

The all-purpose term of affection when you can't remember who you went to bed with the night before, thought Izzy. She felt sick.

She looked round, but she could not see her clothes. His jacket had fallen into a heap just inside the door, though. She picked it up and huddled it round her. The lining had to be silk, from the sensuous way it slithered across her skin. And the coat smelled of sandalwood.

Sandalwood was going to remind her of this man for the rest of her life. She sniffed hard.

A sleepy voice from the bed said, 'Darling?'

Another safely impersonal term of endearment!

'Don't call me darling,' she flashed.

He jack-knifed up in the bed.

'What's going on…?'

Quite suddenly Izzy could not bear it. She was trembling again. But not with passion any more. Not even with laughter. She could not remember that she had ever felt either—not for this man, not for anyone. All she could feel was a great fog of self-disgust.

He got out of bed and padded towards her, unselfconscious in his magnificent nakedness.

'My love, what is it? A bad dream? Tell me.'

A bad dream! Yes, that was what this was. From the moment she'd seen him in those beastly, beastly combats. He was her nightmare, waiting to take her back into the pit of darkness....

He put an arm round her.

'*Don't touch me,*' she said in a voice like honed steel.

Horrified, Dom tore his hands away and stepped back.

'What is it? *What is it?*'

But she was not making any sense. Even Izzy knew it. And that attempted embrace, so touching, so warm, was her undoing. She began to judder like an earthquake and her words fell over themselves. All he could make out was 'third date' and 'whatever I have to'.

Dom could not bear to see her so distressed.

He hooked a chair forward with his foot and urged her into it. He judged that now would not be a good time to touch her. Then he went to the old-fashioned chest of drawers and dug out a decanter. He unstoppered it and sniffed.

'Madeira for Uncle Gerald. God knows how long it's been there.' He poured some into a glass. 'Have a sip anyway.'

She gulped it down like medicine.

'That bad, huh?'

She shook her head. She could not manage a smile. There was a lingering look of horror in her eyes that filled him with dread, though he did not know why.

He pulled a cover off the bed and wrapped it round her shoulders, taking care not to touch her flinching skin. Then he pulled an old robe out of the wardrobe and sat crosslegged on the rug at her feet. He did not attempt to touch her again. But he looked up into her face as gently as a caress.

'Want to tell me what that was about?'

He saw her throat move. Hastily he reached for Uncle's Gerald's Madeira again.

'I knew there had to be a reason for having a dipsomaniac in the family,' he muttered, trying to find some healing laughter. 'The old buffer just justified his existence.'

Izzy tried a smile. It was as pallid as the morning moon out there, though. Dom shook his head, concerned.

What can be this bad? he wondered. Tell me, my love. But he said it silently.

She said with difficulty, 'You're very kind, aren't you?'

'Kind?' said Dom, revolted. 'Me? Nah.'

'You are. I'm sorry. I—should have been straight with you. Only I thought—this time—it didn't seem—'

He held up a hand.

'Hold on there. Transmission breaking up. Can you run that past me again? Starting with the bit where you should have been straight with me. Straight about what?'

Izzy sniffed and knuckled her nose, for all the world like one of yesterday afternoon's penguins, thought Dom.

His eyes lit with tender laughter. He fished a pristine handkerchief from the chest of drawers behind him and handed it over.

She blew her nose loudly. Several times. Then she cleared her throat.

'Sorry. I usually manage better than that.'

His eyebrows knit in a puzzled frown. 'Manage better? Manage what better?'

'Me,' she said baldly. She waved her hand at the bed behind her, although she did not actually look at it. 'Sex. The third date thing. Sorry.'

Suddenly all desire to laugh left Dom. 'The *third date thing*!'

'Um, yes. You know—um—first date you exchange telephone numbers; second date food and drink; third date bodily fluids.' Her voice broke.

Dom did not hear it. All he heard was flippancy. He was outraged.

He said grimly, 'I think you'd better explain.'

'It's not you,' said Izzy hastily. 'It's me. It's all me.'

His mouth tightened dangerously. 'Are you telling me that there's nothing wrong with my technique? Just in case I get a complex?'

Izzy sucked her teeth. That was exactly what she was doing, of course. But it didn't seem to be having the desired effect. In fact, she saw, quite the contrary. He was looking furious.

'Yes. I mean, no. I mean, sorry.' She was floundering.

'Thank you,' said Dom, awfully.

She blew her nose again.

'Look,' she said, goaded. 'I once went to bed with—well, I didn't, but I thought I was going to have to—I—oh, hell!'

He stopped simmering. 'You *what*?' He sounded thunderstruck.

Izzy marshalled her thoughts. This was something she had not told before. She was not sure she could. It would take all her self-control.

She swallowed hard and said in a hard voice in case she cried, 'I was going round the world by bus. You know the sort of thing?'

He nodded, not smiling.

'I'd done it before. I thought I knew the form. I thought I could deal with anything. But— We got stopped by some rebels in a little town in the mountains.' She swallowed. 'They were very jumpy. And—difficult to talk to. Even though I spoke Spanish quite well. They didn't seem to be able to concentrate. Couldn't reason, or something. Anyway, I wasn't getting through.'

His eyes narrowed. 'How many were there of you?'

'A whole busload. The rebels let the locals go. It was only the tourists they hung on to. I told everyone to co-operate. No eye contact. Give them what they want. Keep your head down.'

'You did the right thing.'

'I know. Only—they'd lost their leader and they didn't seem to know what to do next. And one of the men in our party tried to square up to them—' She swallowed, remembering. 'They marched us off into the jungle.'

Dom began to understand. He took both her hands and held them strongly. 'And you got everyone out?'

'Oh, no. It was a joint effort. But I—negotiated.'

'Ah.' His hands tightened comfortingly. 'I've done the negotiation bit myself.'

She didn't say anything.

He let her sit quiet for a minute or two. Then prompted gently, 'I take it sex was one of the bargaining counters?'

She nodded. She didn't look at him. She was twisting and twisting his handkerchief between her fingers and she was concentrating on it as if her life depended on it.

This was where it got difficult. She said, as much to herself as to Dom, 'It's crazy. I didn't even have to do it in the end. They got into a panic and ran away. Just left us there. But somehow, just making up my mind that I would if I had to—' She closed her eyes. Her lips felt numb. From behind her closed eyelids, she said, 'It's stuck—like a splinter that I can't get out.'

'"I do whatever I have to,"' he said slowly, echoing what she had said to him. Was it only yesterday? It felt like another century.

'I—yes.'

'How long ago?'

'Nearly two years.'

'And no third dates ever since?'

She opened her eyes at that. If possible, she looked even more wretched.

'No. No, I—er—I do date. I've got quite good at covering up, as long as I have enough warning.'

He did not understand and said so.

She shook her head, not meeting his eyes. 'You've seen *When Harry Met Sally*? Well, she's right. Orgasm isn't all that hard to do. You cross your eyes and go into an asthma attack.'

There was total silence in the grey morning.

'I see,' he said at last.

She dared a look at him. He was quite expressionless.

'And that's what you do?'

Izzy did not trust her voice. She nodded.

He stood up.

'I see. No wonder you didn't want me to touch you.'

She put a hand over her mouth.

'That was quite a performance you gave last night,' he said, still in that deadly, expressionless voice. 'But it would have been better to say No, thanks, I don't want to, you know.'

Izzy struggled to her feet. The coverlet pooled around her ankles. She clutched the jacket that smelled of him round her so tight that it looked as if she would never give it up.

'I didn't mean it—'

'It's okay. I've grasped that.' The voice lacerated her quivering senses like an ice burn.

'No, you don't understand—' Her voice rose.

'Oh, but I do,' he said gently, and quite, quite icily. 'You don't want to make love. But last

night you tried. Am I supposed to be grateful?'
His bitterness flamed out at her.

Izzy was alarmed. 'No, of course not. I never
meant—'

'Because, you see, I don't want you to try. I
want you to come to me and stay with me and
love me. I don't want you—' Dom's voice rose
in a sudden roar that made her recoil in alarm
'—to cross your eyes and pretend everything is
all right when it clearly isn't. I want the truth.'

Izzy moistened her suddenly dry lips.

'Don't do that,' he said savagely.

'Oh. Um. Sorry. I just wanted you to know the
truth,' said Izzy, shaking but determined.

He sent her a long, unfathomable look which
she couldn't read.

'The truth?'

'Yes.'

'The whole truth?'

'Look, what do you want from me?' she exclaimed. 'I've never told anyone about the—bargain—I made with the rebels. Not even my sister.
No one. But I told you. What more can I do?'

Dom said deliberately, 'Do you or don't you
remember the night I put you to bed?'

'The night—?' Realisation hit. She gave a great
gasp and sat down on the edge of the tumbled
bed. She was very pale.

'Ah,' said Dom. Quite kind. Rather regretful. Implacable as a hanging judge. 'I see you do.'

Her mouth felt as if it wouldn't quite work. 'You know I was the girl in the nightclub. You must know I'm not Jemima, then.' She looked up, suddenly suspicious. 'How long have you known?'

'From the moment you turned up at the jump site.' He put a hand on the doorknob. 'It's odd,' he said reflectively. 'I kept thinking that if you told me why you were impersonating Jemima Dare everything would fall into place and we could walk off hand in hand into the sunset. I was so sure—' He broke off, with a gentle laugh that chilled her to the marrow. 'Still, as you pointed out the whole damned family is a bad judge of women.'

Izzy was utterly silenced.

He opened the door.

'You'll be more comfortable alone,' he said formally.

And was gone.

CHAPTER ELEVEN

Izzy did not sleep for the rest of the cold bleak morning. She wondered if Dom did.

The thoughts went round and round in her head.

She thought, He saw through every pretence, every single evasion, right from the start. I never had a chance.

She thought, I called him *my love*. Not aloud, not in his arms. In my head. Where it's true. Did he know that, too?

And then her more sensible self said, Don't get carried away. He may come on like the lord of the universe. All right, he puts your blood pressure through the roof. The man is, by anybody's standards, fairly gorgeous. He's still just an ordinary man. He is not a superhero and he does not have X-ray vision. Get real, Izzy!

So he wasn't a superhero, and yet he had known from the first that she wasn't Jemima Dare. Account for that, Izzy!

There was only one feasible answer. He and Jemima had to be an item. That crazy dance at the *Out of the Attic* launch hadn't been enough for him to be able to recognise anyone instantly. Especially not across a yard full of photographers the moment she got out of Culp and Christopher's limousine. No matter what he said. He hadn't recognised Izzy. He had simply known she wasn't Jemima.

And yet... And yet...

She had recognised him, hadn't she? She hadn't even known what he looked like but she had recognised him. The pulse of the blood. The scent of sandalwood. The dark chocolate voice that teased or lured, that made love with words as potently as his body made love to hers...

Izzy dressed and sat in a big armchair by the window, watching the sunrise. It was cold. Dom had said it was always cold in English country houses. Izzy hugged her knees to her chest and wanted to laugh and cry at the same time.

How do I know you're not for me? Let me count the ways: my sister saw you first and I don't poach, even if I could. No man in his right mind would look at me when he could have Jemima anyway and I don't see why you would be an exception. You're way out of my league in the gorgeous stakes. And you're a celebrity. And, to cap it all, you're a blasted English aristocrat who knows how to survive in a stately home.

And I lied to you.

But not as much as you think I did.

She knuckled her aching eyes. 'I'm sunk,' she said aloud. 'I'm well and truly sunk. He put his mark on me and I didn't even realise it. What on earth am I going to do now?'

In the morning she looked terrible. Her eyes had great shadows under them. No one noticed.

The kitchen was like Times Square, with people coming, people leaving, people telephoning and leaving messages and some patient woman standing at the big pine table peeling potatoes for a small army.

'Help yourself to coffee, darling,' said the Duchess, waving Izzy towards an industrial-sized pot. 'Dom's gone to pick up Abby.'

'Abby?'

The Duchess raised her pencilled eyebrows. 'You *are* a new acquisition, aren't you?' she said indulgently.

Izzy winced. An acquisition! She nearly said, Not any more. He unloaded me at five o'clock this morning. But the Duchess didn't give her time, and anyway what was the point? The only person who cared was Izzy.

'His sister—Lady Abigail,' explained the Duchess, blithely unaware that Izzy's heart was breaking. 'She's staying with friends a few miles away but she's coming over for the celebration lunch.' She added as an afterthought. 'She has to. She's doing pudding.'

'Oh,' said Izzy, struggling to be polite. 'How nice.'

The coffee tasted as if it had been stewing since the night before. She emptied it down the sink, took a huge glass of water and went out into the garden.

The booths and tents of the day before were still up in the field. But the refreshment tables in the sunken garden had been cleared away. Izzy dropped onto the grass under some luxuriant late roses and tried to sort out a sensible plan of action.

She had to talk to Dom. She had hurt him and been too stupid, in her obsession with looking after Jemima, to see that she was betraying something a lot more important. She had to tell him that she saw that now. She had to make him understand.

Okay, he would probably not forgive her. He certainly did not love her. They might have had a chance, but she had spoilt it all with her wilful determination to stick to the masquerade, come hell or high water.

But she must tell him the truth *now*. She owed it to him. Maybe to both of them. There had been too much lying.

I was not faking when you made me come last night, she said in her head. It didn't even occur to me to fake it. I've been calling you *my love* in my head since the flower meadow.

She went scarlet at the thought. But, scarlet or not, it had to be done. Nobody ever actually dies of embarrassment, she told herself dryly. They just wish they had!

She did not know where she was going to start. Or whether he would listen to her for a minute, let alone through the whole story. It was all too likely that he would never want to see her again. But she had to *try*.

Izzy heard the old Jeep coming up the drive before she saw it. She knew the noise of that engine now as she knew the ring of her mobile phone or the sound of Jemima's laugh. She stood up slowly, took several deep breaths, and went to meet him.

Dom had parked just outside the kitchen again. He was unloading several boxes. When she went up to him he had his head in the back of the vehicle.

'Hello,' she said in a small voice, to the seat of his jeans.

He said impatiently, 'Okay, Abby, I'm going as fast as I can. The damn things won't melt for five more minutes out of the fridge.'

He straightened and saw who it was. At once his face changed like a slate that had been wiped clean. No impatience, no laughter, no curiosity. Just a deadly, deadpan politeness.

'Hello. Did you sleep well?'

Izzy gave a laugh that broke in the middle.

Expression flared into Dom's eyes like a forest fire springing up from nowhere. 'Then maybe we have something to talk about.'

She swallowed. That look was almost too much to bear after she had just been telling herself that he would never want to see her again.

'Please,' she said.

He drew several breaths, as if he had been running. 'Right.' He looked round, distracted. 'Let me get rid of these damned mousses of Abby's and I'll be with you.'

But before he could move a tall woman so like him she had to be his sister came pounding out of the house. She was waving a newspaper. It was, saw Izzy, one of the Sunday tabloids.

'Dom, you did it,' she squealed. 'Aunt Margaret said you did it. It's here in the diary column. Operation Model-Girl Mistress. Oh, I'm so proud of you. Shackleton would have been proud of you. Just wait until we see the other papers...' She trailed off, realising her audience was not with her.

Izzy had thought nothing else could shock her. It seemed she was wrong.

'Operation Model-Girl Mistress?' She was white to the lips.

Abby turned to her eagerly. 'Oh, I'm so sorry. It's a silly publicity stunt my employer cooked up for him. I'm with Culp and Christopher PR.' She thrust out a hand. 'Abby Diz.'

'Isabel Dare,' said Izzy mechanically. She let Abby seize her hand and pump it energetically. She did not look at Dom. She gave a bright, bright smile aimed at the middle distance and hoped that she could get away before she was actually physically sick. 'A PR stunt, eh? I've heard about those. Never been part of one before, though.'

'Part—?' Abby looked to her brother for help. 'I don't understand.'

'I'll explain later,' he said, not taking his eyes off Izzy. 'For now, just get lost, Ab, there's a good girl.'

'But my puddings—'

He stepped back from the car with an expansive gesture. 'Are all yours.'

He took Izzy by the elbow and walked her away from the house. She remembered that grip.

He had held her like that when he walked her out of the nightclub.

'A PR stunt?' she said again. She felt stunned. She sounded it, even to her own ears.

Dom said urgently, 'It's not as crude as it sounds—'

But Izzy was groping her way through this new betrayal. 'I was going to come and grovel,' she said blankly. 'I was going to tell you that I've always looked after my sister Jemima, since she was a baby. That I know when she is in trouble. That's how I knew it was bad this time. I was trying to give her a breathing space to get her life back together when—' She broke off, suddenly looking up at him. 'But none of that matters, does it? As long as I posed for the cameras you didn't care sixpence who I was or why I was doing it.'

'*No,*' he cried.

But she swept on. 'To think I was going to apologise! To you. And you set me up for a—*publicity*—stunt?' She could hardly get the words out.

'No,' said Dom quietly.

'I *hate* you,' yelled Izzy.

She was nearly dancing with rage. She fed the flames deliberately. Rage was a lot, lot better than the other thing that was waiting to break out.

Betrayal. Once she let herself feel his betrayal she was going to drown.

Dom marched her down to a secluded corner surrounded by laurel hedges. They could not see the house. The house could not see them.

Izzy hardly noticed. She was shaking with re-action.

Dom took her by the shoulders and swung her round to face him. 'Listen to me, Izzy. That *is* your name? Izzy?'

She nodded. Little tremors kept rippling through her like the tide. Mostly anger. *Please let it be anger—until I'm alone.*

'Right. That's one step forward, then. Listen to me. The daft bats that run Culp and Christopher kept talking to me about getting column inches on the celebrity circuit and I kept telling them to forget it. And then I saw you—and all I could think of was finding you again.'

Izzy was still breathing hard. 'Then why didn't you?'

He clutched his hair. 'Because you didn't have so much as a credit card in that damned red hand-bag. I hadn't a clue who you were. I tried to ask—but the only woman who knew had gone out of town, blast her. Everyone else had helpful suggestions. Lots of helpful suggestions. I was working my way through the list when I found you again.'

Izzy said flatly. 'I don't believe it.'

'I know you don't,' Dom said in despair. 'I don't know how to convince you.' His eyes were wild but he was making great efforts to stay rational. 'How do you think I knew you weren't Jemima? Everyone else was taken in.'

'You're lovers?' suggested Izzy, her eyes narrowed to evil slits in case she cried.

Dom looked appalled. 'You can't think that!'

'You know her,' she said unanswerably. 'She knows you.'

A muscle beat in Dom's jaw. 'Yes. Because, my darling, I sat next to your sister Jemima for several hours at a charity ball. She's a skinny kid, quite sweet in her way. But I'd never have manhandled her into a taxi and taken her off to have my wicked way with her, like I did you.'

'What?'

He took hold of her again. 'What I did that night—what I've been doing these last three days—it is so unlike me none of my friends, none of my family would believe it if I told them. I wouldn't have done it for Jemima. I wouldn't have done it for anyone else. Izzy—'

The look in his eyes made her head swim. Quite suddenly she thought, Maybe I can trust him after all. Maybe I can even convince him to trust me.

'I knew as soon as you stuck your leg between my thighs on that damned dance floor,' he said simply.

Izzy felt her ears go scarlet.

'I love the way they do that,' said Dom, distracted.

'Stop it,' she shouted, clapping her hands to the side of her face.

'Yes, all right,' he said hastily. 'Look it wasn't just sex, Izzy. I've had lots of that and it's great. But it doesn't grab you by the throat and make you think about nothing else. All I wanted, from the moment you ran out on me, was to find you again. And make you stay the night.' He grimaced. 'And then when I did—'

Izzy put her hands on his chest. 'Don't.'

He looked tortured. 'I have to. Let me say this now, Izzy. I need to—get it out, somehow. I love you. I don't know why or how it happened. I just know it has. And if you won't have me—well, it doesn't make any difference. I still love you.'

'Oh,' said Izzy humbled. 'But why didn't you tell me?'

'Why didn't *you* tell *me*?' he countered. 'I gave you opportunity after opportunity to tell me you weren't Jemima. You never trusted me.'

'Yes, I did,' said Izzy quietly.

'Hell, I even took a gamble and trusted you with my own big secret. I thought it might encourage you to reciprocate. But—it didn't work. Nothing worked.' His face looked thin and pinched.

She stared. Then realised what his secret must be. 'The book you can't write,' she said, on a wondering note.

He nodded. 'No one knows how bad the dyslexia is. Though I'm going to be found out soon. No one can understand why I won't write a book about the Antarctic trip.'

An idea occurred to her. 'Now you mention it—'

'I'm not going to let you get me off the subject,' he said fiercely. 'Izzy, I need you to know that I never wanted to use you. Never intended to use you. The only people who were getting used were Culp and Christopher. They seemed to be my only point of contact with you.'

'But I've got a really great idea. You could—'

'Stop it,' he shouted, rocked out of his English gentleman's cool for the first time since she had known him. '*Listen* to me. I would have stripped naked and walked on fire if that's what it took to find you again. A publicity stunt was nothing. I would have done anything.'

She'd wondered what would happen if he decided to stop being a gentleman, Izzy remembered suddenly. Well, now she knew. He took possession of her heart.

She said quietly, 'I love you. And I want to write your Antarctic book.'

That stopped him as nothing else would have done.

'Izzy—'

'You can dictate messages for me, can't you? Even if you don't want to dictate for a publisher?'

He looked shaken to the heart. 'I'll dictate you a love letter every day. I'll even try my hand at damned poetry if that's what you want.' He grabbed her hands and held them strongly.

'Izzy,' he said with difficulty, 'I'm not a great bet. I disappear off into wild places for months at a time. I've never read a sonnet in my life. And my family dress up as penguins. But I know your secrets. And you know mine. I think we need each other.'

The scent of roses filled the air. But all Izzy could smell was sandalwood. Sandalwood was going to mean happiness to her for the rest of her life.

A great laugh began to bubble up. 'You mean you'll settle for a mistress who isn't a model girl after all?' she said, looking at him from under her lashes. 'Are you going to tell the papers you fell over me by accident?'

Dom narrowed his eyes at her. 'Accident be blowed. I worked damned hard to fall over you.'

'*The Accidental Mistress,*' she mused naughtily. 'Nice headline. It's got something.'

But Dom was back on form again. He gave her one of his bland smiles. 'But I kept telling Culp and Christopher. I don't want a mistress.'

Izzy was taken aback. Suddenly all her lovely confidence fell away, leaving her once again the sister who wasn't the pretty one, the third wheel, the one a man only made love to by accident. 'Don't you?' she said uncertainly.

He shook his head. 'But if you care to change the offer...?' he suggested.

'Change it?' She was lost.

'I could,' he said magnificently, 'be persuaded into marriage.'

'Oh,' said Izzy.

There was a stunned silence.

Dom lost some of his magnificence. 'It doesn't have to be at once. If you need time, I mean. I'm certain, but I can see that you may not be—' He broke off. 'What are you doing?'

Izzy looked up innocently. 'I thought I'd take my clothes off,' she explained helpfully. She started to unbutton Jemima's crisp cotton shirt.

'As we got in such a pickle last night, I thought it might be a good thing if I started it this time.'

Dom went very still. 'You don't have to prove anything to me,' he said quietly. 'Whatever the problems, we'll sort them out together.'

'Good,' said Izzy. 'But one problem we don't have.' She let the shirt drop to the grass.

Dom swallowed. The grey-green eyes were intent and very serious.

Izzy put her hand on the zip of her jeans. It was half a challenge. Half something a lot more than that. And they both knew it.

Izzy did the long, lingering come-and get-me look that Jemima had shown her. She gave it her best shot.

It seemed to work. Dom's head went back. He looked thunderstruck.

She began to feel better. 'Do you think this would persuade you?' she asked in an interested voice. 'To marry me, I mean?'

'You mean—' he sounded stunned '—you will? Just like that? I don't have to write poetry or do twelve months' hard labour or anything? I don't have to *try*?'

'No,' said Izzy.

It did not seem as if he could believe it.

Izzy stopped fiddling with her jeans and straightened her shoulders. She looked him straight in the eye and tried not to think about her semaphore ear colour.

'I have,' she said bravely, 'been calling you my love in my head for the last twenty-four hours. And last night I could not keep my hands off you.'

His eyes glinted. 'I remember. Though I was beginning to think it was an illusion.'

'No illusion. I think,' said Izzy in her most businesslike tone, though she knew her ears must be incandescent, 'you've covered all the salient points. Don't think there's anything left to do.'

'Oh, yes there is,' said Dom, his eyes glinting wickedly. 'Bring those jeans over here. *Now.*'

Izzy laughed. And then she gave a great sigh and walked into the shelter of her lover's arms.

They made it to the celebration lunch by the skin of their teeth. Izzy's shirt, thought Dom with satisfaction, was looking very pleasantly rumpled, in spite of the fact that they had both applied their attention to making sure that it was properly buttoned before they came back into the house. Izzy had wanted to change, but Dom felt a fondness for that shirt and had wanted her to keep it on.

So Izzy had laughed and said, 'Right you are. If it makes you feel good.'

He ran a finger up her spine in a way which
he was learning made her shiver voluptuously.

'I wouldn't say *good*, exactly,' he murmured.

Izzy thumped him companionably. 'Behave.
We've got a lot of explaining to do.'

Dom looked astonished.

'We have.' She looked nervous suddenly. 'I'm
here under false pretences, after all.'

'Leave that to me,' said Dom, his magnificent
assurance restored. 'I know how to handle my
family.'

So she should not have been surprised now,
when he tinged his glass with a fork to bring the
table to silence just as his sister was about to
serve her collection of puddings.

'Three things,' said Dom crisply. 'One, the
woman you thought was Jemima is her sister
Izzy.' He barely paused, simply talking over the
top of the intrigued buzz. 'Two, I'm in love with
her. Three, I'm going to marry her.'

Izzy choked.

Dom sat back, well pleased. There was total
silence.

His sister looked at Izzy hard. 'Is this true?'

'Yes,' said Izzy with total confidence.

'All of it?'

After her morning in the rose garden she was
never going to doubt that Dom loved her again.

She reached her hand to him across the table. 'All
of it,' said Izzy softly.

Dom took her hand. His eyes were so full of
love that he hardly looked the same man. 'Good,'
he said, smiling into her eyes with an alluring
combination of promise and shared memory.
'That's two puds for everyone, please, Abby.
We've got a second engagement to celebrate.'

MILLS & BOON® PUBLISH EIGHT LARGE PRINT TITLES A MONTH. THESE ARE THE EIGHT TITLES FOR MARCH 2004

❧

THE ITALIAN BOSS'S MISTRESS
Lynne Graham

THE BEDROOM SURRENDER
Emma Darcy

A SPANISH VENGEANCE
Diana Hamilton

THE MILLIONAIRE'S VIRGIN MISTRESS
Robyn Donald

THE ACCIDENTAL MISTRESS
Sophie Weston

THE BRIDE ASSIGNMENT
Leigh Michaels

THE MARRIAGE COMMAND
Susan Fox

A SURPRISE CHRISTMAS PROPOSAL
Liz Fielding

MILLS & BOON®

Live the emotion

0204